VALENTINE'S WITH THE SILVER FOX

AVA GRAY

Copyright © 2025 by Ava Gray

All rights reserved.

No part of this book may be reproduced in any form or by any electronic or mechanical means, including information storage and retrieval systems, without written permission from the author, except for the use of brief quotations in a book review.

❀ Created with Vellum

ALSO BY AVA GRAY

CONTEMPORARY ROMANCE

Mafia Kingpins Series

His to Own

His to Protect

His to Win

His to Possess

The Valkov Bratva Series

Stolen by the Bratva

Kept by the Bratva

Captured by the Bratva

Captivated by the Bratva

. . .

AVA GRAY

Festive Flames Series

Silver Hills' Christmas Miracle

Holly, Jolly, and Oh So Naughty

The Christmas Eve Delivery

Valentine's with the Silver Fox

Harem Hearts Series

3 SEAL Daddies for Christmas

Small Town Sparks

Her Protector Daddies

Her Alpha Bosses

The Mafia's Surprise Gift

The Billionaire Mafia Series

Knocked Up by the Mafia

Stolen by the Mafia

Claimed by the Mafia

Arranged by the Mafia

Charmed by the Mafia

Alpha Billionaire Series

Secret Baby with Brother's Best Friend

Just Pretending

Loving The One I Should Hate

Billionaire and the Barista

Coming Home

Doctor Daddy

Baby Surprise

A Fake Fiancée for Christmas

Hot Mess

Love to Hate You - The Beckett Billionaires

Just Another Chance - The Beckett Billionaires

Valentine's Day Proposal

The Wrong Choice - Difficult Choices

The Right Choice - Difficult Choices

SEALed by a Kiss

The Boss's Unexpected Surprise

Twins for the Playboy

When We Meet Again

The Rules We Break

Secret Baby with my Boss's Brother

Frosty Beginnings

Silver Fox Billionaire

Taken by the Major

Daddy's Unexpected Gift

Off Limits

AVA GRAY

Boss's Baby Surprise

CEO's Baby Scandal

Playing with Trouble Series:

Chasing What's Mine

Claiming What's Mine

Protecting What's Mine

Saving What's Mine

The Beckett Billionaires Series:

Love to Hate You

Just Another Chance

Standalone's:

Ruthless Love

The Best Friend Affair

PARANORMAL ROMANCE

Maple Lake Shifters Series:

Omega Vanished

Omega Exiled

Omega Coveted

Omega Bonded

Everton Falls Mated Love Series:

The Alpha's Mate

The Wolf's Wild Mate

Saving His Mate

Fighting For His Mate

Dragons of Las Vegas Series:

Thin Ice

Silver Lining

A Spark in the Dark

Fire & Ice

Dragons of Las Vegas Boxed Set (The Complete Series)

Standalone's:

Fiery Kiss

Wild Fate

BLURB

One desperate night sealed our fate.

He's a silver fox tech billionaire.

I'm just the girl hired to save his marriage...

Distinguished and powerful.

Devastatingly handsome.

Like temptation in a thousand-dollar suit.

His wife left him without warning.

Now he wants me to transform their vow renewal ceremony...

Into the party where he'll announce their divorce.

EXCEPT...

One night of passion turned into more.

Now he's making me an offer I can't refuse.

Two million dollars to chase my dreams.

The man who could make or break my future.

And I can't stop craving his touch.

This party could launch my career.

At least that's what I keep telling myself.

Till a pregnancy test changes everything.

And he takes the stage to make an announcement.

One that will destroy us both.

Some Valentine's gifts come with life-changing consequences...

And this silver fox is about to discover just how permanent our little "business arrangement" really is.

Author's Note: *A steamy age-gap romance featuring a silver fox billionaire, an unexpected pregnancy, and a Valentine's surprise you won't see coming. Get ready. This February is about to heat up!*

1

JAMES

I locked my phone and slid it into my pocket. The text I had been waiting for all day had finally come in and I was tense. After the argument Barbra and I had this morning, I held out almost no hope that my plan would be successful. I tried to keep my chin high, staring out the window at the snow that blanketed everything and covered the iced-over bay. It felt like I'd been unsuccessful at the one thing in life I never thought I had to worry about.

My business was successful. I'd poured years into developing the latest AI models that were now reaching global scales and growing in leaps and bounds. But my marriage was in shambles, if you could even call it a marriage. Barbra had been on again, off again for the past year, but mostly "off" for the past six months.

Ms. Hart was supposed to help me change that. I paid a huge fee for her services, and while she was no marriage therapist—just a wedding planner—I had heard she was a miracle worker, the best in the business. My attempt at wooing Barbra back from the brink of divorce just in time for the holidays, with a Valentine's Day vow renewal ceremony, was a grand gesture I hoped Barbra would see as romantic and thoughtful.

I turned away from the window and headed out of my office and down the long hallway toward the living room. The whole place had shifted and transformed in the past five days. As soon as Halloween was over, my staff went to work decorating for the season of thanks, and my entire eight-bedroom home was now drenched in hues of orange, yellow, and brown—something Barbra had always insisted on.

I wasn't much of a decorator, though I liked things to look nice. She was the one who took care of it all, and the staff always acted as an extension of her very own hands. I appreciated that about her, and in that way, she was a good partner. She softened my edges a little and made our house feel like home, despite the utter lack of familial feelings in the massive home. She'd never wanted children, and since it was her body, I had no choice. Another sore spot between us.

Maybe that was why she cheated. It'd been a year since I walked in and found her with her personal trainer doing moves I'd never even seen before, let alone thought were possible. She craved a life I wasn't giving her, and I focused on my empire and the future I thought it would buy for Barbra and me. I hadn't laid a hand on her since then, mostly because of her choices. I wanted to make things right. She didn't.

But I wasn't going to stop trying. When I said, "'Til death do us part," I meant it. Better or worse turned out to be a lot worse than I thought, and six months of therapy didn't help. She swore she wasn't with the man anymore, and I believed her, but her jaunts to hotels around the country for two or three weeks at a time to "clear her head and think" had gotten more regular. Now I was beginning to wonder if my money was just affording her the luxury to have multiple partners in multiple states.

I nervously checked my phone again, but there were no new updates. If Ms. Hart could work miracles, then possibly Barbra would begin to see that I really did want to put as much effort into this as possible. Things had been so dead and dry for so long, there really was so little hope that anyone could restore things quickly, but with a little effort, I thought we could start over.

I heard noise behind me and turned toward the arched door between the front entryway and the living room and noticed Barbra walking in with two suitcases. She wore a purple suit and black heels. Her hair was tucked under a hat, and she wore her coat, hanging open in the front.

She turned to look at me, and her expression was void of any emotion or indication of what was happening. "James," she said, stepping into the living room and standing at the fringed edge of the Persian rug.

"Are you going somewhere?" I asked, confused at why she had suitcases. She'd only just returned yesterday from two weeks on the east coast, and I thought she intended to stay for the holidays. We had several parties and gatherings we traditionally hosted, things our friends and family members looked forward to each year. She was the one who started the tradition, and I thought she enjoyed entertaining.

"Yes," she said curtly. As she spoke, she started to zip up her coat.

"Well, where are you going? How long will you be gone? We have a lot of planning to do for—"

"I'm leaving, James." Barbra's head rose and she locked eyes with me, and I knew exactly what she meant without further explanation, but I just wasn't willing to accept it. It was like she quit a long time ago, and I knew she'd quit, but I kept going through the motions. Maybe that was how she felt when I was working so much and she was waiting for me to come home and spend time with her. I understood that much. It just didn't excuse the cheating.

"Well, when will you be back?" I took a hesitant step toward her and thought about how I'd heard her say these words so many times that my heart even stopped responding. I felt cold and dead inside, not panicked or angry or insecure in the least. I felt calm.

"I'm not coming back." Her chin lifted slightly when she said it, her nose in the air. The determined expression she wore told me she'd made her choice now and no matter what I said or did, she wasn't going to change her mind.

"I see..." Anger wanted to rise up, but I pushed it down. We'd argued so much, there were no words left to scream at each other, no mud to sling, no blame to be placed. I neglected her. She cheated on me and broke my heart and my ability to trust. I wanted to work it out. She wanted freedom. It was that simple.

"An annulment would be easiest," she said as she turned to pick up her bags. I heard car tires crunch the snow and ice out front and looked out to see a car pull up. "If you just sign the damn papers the first time, we won't have a lengthy court battle." She stooped and wrapped her hands around the handles of the suitcases and lifted them. "Get the door," she ordered, and I scowled.

But I did what she wanted. Strangely, this announcement didn't surprise or disappoint me. I walked toward the door and put my hand on the knob and sighed. "And you're certain there is nothing I can say or do to change your mind?" When I saw the look of anger and contempt on her face, I pulled the door open and stepped back.

She walked past me without a word and out into the crisp November air and toward her car, her driver waiting with the engine running. She'd been planning this all morning, probably since the argument, and I'd naively come downstairs to prepare for Ms. Hart's arrival with the thought that it was just another argument, just another day of misery. Now Barbra was climbing into her limo and Ms. Hart was exiting her Uber, and they passed each other on the sidewalk.

Ms. Hart smiled, but I know Barbra only scowled at her. It was the only expression I'd seen on Barbra's face in six months. I knew it well. She had turned into a very bitter, angry woman I hardly recognized, and I had lost all respect or affection for her. My actions had been out of duty—the sanctity of marriage as an institution, my morals, what I was taught to believe. And I was a fool for trying long after she'd given up.

"Uh, hello…" Ms. Hart stood on my front stoop, layered in winter gear with rosy cheeks and nose, and her hand reached out toward me. "I'm Ivy Hart, here to consult for your vow renewal service in February."

I looked down at her hand blankly and robotically took it and shook it. I felt hollow, like Barbra had taken an ice cream scoop and dug my insides out and thrown them away. I wanted to tell Ms. Hart her services weren't needed. Hell, I'd have let her keep the full fee and move on, but I didn't want to be alone right now. I knew if I went into that huge house that was now empty—permanently—my anger would get the better of me and I'd go into a spiral.

I looked down at her hand in mine and blinked slowly, then nodded and stepped aside as I let her go. "Please come in…" I now had zero hope that Barbra and I were ever getting back together, and the truth was somehow freeing. It felt like I could stop pretending to want something that felt like more work than it was worth. Though, the idea of navigating the holidays alone for the first time in fifteen years felt daunting.

I followed Ms. Hart into my living room and shut the door. She began to unbundle herself, and I didn't even know how to tell her the entire event was probably off. My life was off. My heart was off, and I just felt defeated.

"You have a lovely home," she said, and she peeled her coat off and draped it over her arm. She wore a mustard-colored sweater and a black skirt. Her long brown hair was braided and draped across her shoulder, and her heart-shaped face was endearing. She had a welcoming smile too, something that always appealed to me.

"Thank you… Um, Ms. Hart, I'm afraid my plans for the vow renewal have just changed." I walked toward the center of the room and gestured at my leather sofa. "Please have a seat." I sat down in the leather armchair nearest the fireplace as she situated herself at the end of the sofa, and I thought of how without Barbra, there was no reason for the event in February, no way I'd pull off my holiday obligations either. Unless Ms. Hart could magically transform from a wedding planner to an event coordinator.

"Changed?" she said, and apprehension knit her brow. Unlike Barbra's stoic face, easily able to hide any emotion, Ms. Hart wore her feelings on her sleeve.

I knew I was under contract with her, and she probably counted on this job. I had already paid for the entire thing, though the venue was non-refundable, and while I didn't care about the wasted money, I hated the wasted effort. A plan started to form in my mind as I stewed over how Barbra had left me so suddenly. I'd never done all the holiday prep myself. I needed someone who knew what they were doing.

"Ms. Hart, would you stay for lunch? I think I have a proposition you might be interested in—if it fits into your schedule." I watched her face shift from nervous to curious, and she nodded.

"Of course. I'd be happy to hear your proposal."

Proposal... now that was a word that cut me deep. Changing my surprise vow renewal to something more depressing while navigating a barren holiday season was the farthest thing from a proposal than I'd ever care to feel. I hoped Ms. Hart could still be my magic charm. Maybe she'd make the holidays bearable, at the very least.

2

IVY

It wasn't abnormal to dine with a client and discuss event plans. What was out of the ordinary was how Mr. Carver hosted this meal in his own dining room with his own staff catering to my every whim.

We had ham and potato soup with freshly made bread and butter, and the wine the maid brought out probably cost more than my entire wardrobe. After living in a hotel for the past two months in search of an affordable apartment here in Lover's Bay, the meal and the company were both a very nice change of pace. But we hadn't even said one thing about the vow renewal I was paid to plan for Mr. Carver and his wife, and my bowl and my glass were empty.

I didn't want to be rude. He took a lot of time asking me questions about my experience and what sort of weddings I'd planned. When he got to the part about my business partner, I cringed, but I was honest. Mike was a total jerk and I wanted nothing to do with him. In fact, I was taking my clients and leaving and the partnership was dissolving too. It didn't bode well for me as far as picking up new clients went since Mike did most of the marketing, but Mr. Carver's party was supposed to help jumpstart my new startup.

"Well, that's a huge undertaking," he said, and he folded his hands under his chin and looked very thoughtful as he rested his elbows on the table on either side of his empty bowl.

"Yeah," I said, sighing. I wasn't going to confess how down I'd been about things or my fears about starting over. But I did have my worries. I was a wedding planner. Normal, everyday people didn't hire wedding planners because weddings were very expensive. Which meant I'd have to cater to the wealthy elite, and they weren't so easy to hook.

"I take it you've had a falling out?" Mr. Carver's slight prying was a little uncomfortable, and I didn't want him to get the idea that just because I was leaving the firm, I didn't know what I was doing. I was the backbone of the entire thing. If anything, Mike was going to lose customers and would have to hire someone new to replace me. I was the one with talent.

"Well, unfortunately, yes." My admission was quiet but honest. When Mr. Carver said something about changing the plan, I had a mini panic attack inside. I had already spent the past two months planning everything down to the most meticulous details. I was ready to go over things and get a team together to finish things up within his budget. I didn't have time to make changes to an event plan still months out. I had to secure more clients between now and then to fill my time and put money in my bank account. I needed an apartment.

"I see... Sounds like we're both in similar straits..." The storm that was in his expression when I first arrived returned. My gut told me that severe-looking woman who was walking out when I was walking in was the reason for it, though I wasn't sure why.

"Similar straits?" I repeated and offered a confused expression. Other than the fact that Mr. Carver wanted to keep his vow renewal a surprise for now, I knew nothing about him. He was rich—some tech mogul or something—and he lived in a massive home that had three living rooms, two dining rooms, and from what I'd read on the internet, something like eight or ten bedrooms. And he had no children.

With money like that, he could afford the Jean George for catering—if he lived that close. I was too modest in my first budget estimate and I should've asked for more. But growing up in a middle-class family in the Midwest, I actually learned to be ultra frugal and I made the inexpensive look lavish.

"I'm just going to be honest with you, Ms. Hart. My wife and I are separating. My hopes to spend the next few months with her rekindling our flame didn't pan out. I had every intention of asking her to renew our vows on Christmas Day and go ahead in February as planned, and well..." He pursed his lips and looked away with just his eyes, and I began to realize what had happened.

That woman storming out must've been Mrs. Carver leaving. I wondered about the suitcases and the glare she shot me. That was so heartbreaking for him, and I wanted to give him a big hug to comfort him. But he was just a client—albeit a very good-looking and ruggedly handsome client.

"I'm so sorry to hear that." Now I understood the reason he wanted to change the event, and I knew why. He was going to ask me to do something entirely different or he was going to cancel, and then what would I do? And after I'd spent some of his money already on a hotel room for the past two months.

"I'm leveling with you because I think you can help me." Mr. Carver sat back in his seat and folded his hands over his lap. I didn't know how a wedding planner could help him with his relationship problems, but I was willing to listen to him. If that was her just leaving, he probably had some things he wanted to get off his chest.

"How do you feel I can best help you?" I sat back too, preparing myself for whatever he might say. I'd had clients ask me to be a mediator between them and their partners before, and while I wasn't a psychologist, I was always willing to help with healthy communication—something Mike and I failed at.

He breathed in deeply and then sighed before he continued. "I'm not surprised that Barbra left. The marriage has been in shambles for the past year or better. She blames me. I accept my part in it, but honestly, we were going nowhere fast. My last-ditch attempt was a hail Mary and it failed. I can't even say I blame her for being unhappy, but she did some unacceptable things. That said, I have no time to wallow in pity. I've done enough grieving over this relationship in the past nine months to last me a lifetime.

"My holiday schedule, however, won't be put on hold. I host dinners and events throughout all of November and December, and I am nothing if not impotent when it comes to party planning. I wonder, Ms. Hart, have you ever done any party planning that wasn't specifically centered around weddings?" Mr. Carver's eyebrows went up as he examined me, and I swallowed hard and licked my lips.

I wasn't necessarily a party planner, per se, but it wasn't that much more difficult than wedding planning. I had a system for weddings, vendors, caterers, heaps of resources all around nuptials. But I did plan rehearsal dinners, bridal showers, and bachelor/bachelorette parties for my clients too. Those were all parties—not quite holiday get-togethers, but mostly the same idea.

"Well, sir, you may be in luck. The situation I'm in is quite difficult too." I looked down and pressed my lips into a line before I looked back up at him. He was being honest with me, and I felt like I owed it to him to be honest with him. He needed someone, and I was the someone he chose.

"As I told you earlier, my former partner and I are dissolving the partnership. I get to retain the clients I have on my list, while he keeps his. I am in a sort of rebranding mode for myself and my ideas for what I'll be doing with my knowledge and expertise." I heard my voice crack since I basically wasn't an expert at anything but weddings. "And you might just be able to help me a little too. What do you have in mind?"

Mr. Carver smiled and leaned forward. As he outlined all the things I'd have to do—Thanksgiving dinners for personal and private parties, holiday galas, Christmas events, gift coordination for corporate shareholders and employees—I started to feel overwhelmed. It was a lot for any one person to do, and I wasn't sure if I was up to the task until he said, "Barbra used to do it all, but she's gone now."

My sympathy rankled any chance I had of bowing out of such an enormous undertaking, and I smiled softly. "Don't worry, Mr. Carver, you're in good hands. I'll be able to handle all of this for you. I'll just need a dedicated workspace, a budget to hire a team to work with, and access to funds to make it happen. I can draw up a budget for each event, starting with those nearest in time, and have it to you in a few days. Then we can go from there..."

He smiled for the first time, and though I knew it was because I'd just saved him from a headache this winter, part of me felt like it was just for me.

"Thank you, Ms. Hart."

"Call me Ivy. We'll be getting to know each other pretty well over the next few months." I wished I had just one more glass of wine to take the nerves off as he stood and asked me to follow him. He led me through the maze of rooms toward a wing of his house that was dark and cold and opened a series of doors—a bedroom, then what appeared to be an office, a bathroom, and a walk-in closet that was larger than my hotel room. Then he turned to me with confidence.

"You'll have all of this space and more if you need it. And you can feel free to stay here as much or as little as you'd like to ensure you can do the job well. That's all I want—excellence in everything. I'll get you a company credit card, and whatever budget you set, I'll sign off on it immediately. You have no idea how thankful I am for you."

My head spun and I felt a little lightheaded. He was approving my budget before I even gave an estimate. And the idea of staying here instead of paying that huge nightly amount for the hotel wasn't half bad, either. I'd have way more space and privacy. It seemed Mr. Carver was a godsend to me as much as I was one to him.

I stretched out my hand and shook his. "I can't wait to get started." As nervous as I was, I knew this was going to put me back on the map, and maybe I could entirely rebrand as a party planner and strengthen my chances of being successful.

Not bad at all.

3

JAMES

"It's only been eight days, though. Maybe she'll change her mind." Sam, my best friend and business partner, sat across from me at the conference table at headquarters. I knew he meant well, but he was wrong. Sam and I had been through hell and back with this company, and he'd even managed to forge a friendship with Barbra over the years too. He just didn't know her like I did.

"I'm afraid you're wrong this time, Sam." I sat back in the leather chair, and it squeaked as it reclined slightly. Sun poured in the picture windows and bathed the room in light, but it did nothing to lighten my mood. "I got served less than twenty-four hours after she was gone. They're not even divorce papers. With the prenup, she knows she will get only the fifty grand up front and five grand a month in alimony. She wants an annulment, and I think she's got someone else lined up to marry her immediately. She can't live without money."

Sam scowled and bounced the back of his seat in a rocking motion as he shook his head. "You think she was just in it for the money the whole time, then?"

I'd thought about that too, that maybe Barbra was always just a gold digger and would never be anything but. Except it didn't jive with the reason we fell apart. I gave her everything she wanted from the very beginning. She didn't cheat because of a lack of money. She cheated because of a lack of intimacy, for which I was partially to blame.

"Nah, I don't think that's the case. If so, she'd have contested the prenup." My eyes roamed over the conference room. Only moments ago, it had been full of shareholders and board members and we had given a presentation to beat them all. But the instant they were gone, Sam cornered me. He knew me too well to let this bad mood continue.

"I'm sorry, man..." He looked thoughtful for a moment and then narrowed his eyes at me. "Does this mean that fancy gala you planned for renewing your vows is off? Bethany was really excited about that. She had me buy this fancy couture gown." He rolled his eyes and chuckled. His wife was a dear friend of ours, and I knew how much she was looking forward to it. All of our friends were. We were planning the surprise of the century, and now it would likely turn out to be just a Valentine's party for adults with nothing to do but put on expensive clothing and drink pricy champagne.

"I'm not canceling it. It's going forward. By then, I should have my final release and I'll use that party as a means to make sure all of my friends know at the same time. That way, I don't have to tell the same story a million times." I raked a hand across my face and thought of Ms. Hart, currently settling into her new room at my home. I had no idea she had been living in a hotel after leaving her former partner, and having her things picked up and brought to my place felt bittersweet. We were more alike than I cared to admit.

"Really? Well, Bethany will be thrilled. What about Christmas and—"

"Everything is still on. I hired a party planner. Barbra cheated on me, Sam. I might not have been as attentive as I should've been, but when I saw what I did that hurt her, I tried. We did counseling, and I was willing to do anything, even forgive her infidelity. But her leaving is the right thing. I stopped loving her the instant she told me she'd been seeing that asshole for six months. Any respect I had for her is gone." I felt my chest tighten in anger. I thought I'd actually let go of it, but I hadn't.

"Well, it's a good attitude to have. A planner is a good thing too. I know Barbra used to do all of that." Sam stood up and buttoned his suit jacket, and I knew our little gab fest was coming to a close. We both had work to get done.

"That's all Barbra has been to me in a year, anyway. A party planner. It's time to move on. Who knows? Maybe love will strike again someday, but I'm not holding my breath." I stood too, shaking his hand before saying, "Top golf on Saturday?" Our tradition of hitting the indoor range wasn't going to change, either.

"Wouldn't miss it. Winner buys the brews at the pub." He winked at me and turned to go, and I chuckled.

I would have to learn to function without a wife, and it would take time to rearrange my life again, but I'd move on and I'd be better for it. The more I told myself that, the better I felt and the more I looked forward to doing the holidays a new way. Maybe Ms. Hart was my lucky charm, after all.

4

IVY

The room was packed. When James told me I could have this massive space to do his planning and organizing for all the events he had slated for me to host, I thought I'd have more than enough space, but I underestimated what I would need. Kevin, my right-hand man, stood by the mood board checking out color palettes and swatches. Thanksgiving was an easy one—orange, brown, and yellow. But I had so many events, it only seemed fitting to offer each one my full attention and a unique idea.

"I'm not sure, hun. The lighter shades just aren't gelling with my vision." Kevin shook his head and stepped back, and I set my timeline diagram aside and stepped up next to him.

"I think it's great. I'm not seeing what you dislike. This is the same scheme we used to decorate the offices last year." I glanced at his expression, which was clearly a sign that he was grossed out.

"I know, but it's really so last year. I think we should go with darker browns and warmer oranges. You know the vendors are going to have a hard time sourcing things in this lighter shade." He clicked his tongue and turned to peer over the seating chart next. He was my biggest critic, but I paid him to be that. He really had an eye for this stuff even if we didn't see eye to eye every time.

I picked up a swatch and thought about what he was saying, and maybe he was right. I'd had a challenging time sourcing everything last year too. But I just loved the lighter colors and I wanted everything to be perfect.

"This seating chart is too complicated. You should just be simple, girl. No one wants to be told where to sit." He turned a skeptical eye on me and scowled. I might have agreed with him when it came to colors, but I knew my clients. A seating chart was something the Carvers did every year. I spoke with his staff, and I knew what his guests would expect.

"No, I don't agree. I put this together based on every other party he's hosted. I know what I'm doing. I want James to look really good, Kevin. His wife just walked out of his life a few weeks ago and he's going through stuff. This has to be perfect." I put the swatch down and walked toward the stack of paperwork so I could find my vendor and supplier charts. If Kevin thought the colors I wanted would be hard to source, then I needed to get on the orders right now. Who knew how long shipping would take.

"I don't see why you're even doing this. Thanksgiving parties aren't your thing, Ivy. You're a wedding planner," he said in a sing-song voice. He spun in a circle in a very dramatic way and sighed. "You love doing weddings. Why would you rebrand your entire company to do parties? One minute you're planning Thanksgiving for the wealthy, and the next thing you know, you're fishing some six-year-old out of a ball pit in a smelly, germ-infested playground for a birthday party."

He rolled his eyes and slumped onto the chair next to the roll-top desk in the corner of the room. James's decorator was fantastic. I couldn't have made this room more beautiful myself, definitely not as prim and proper. I felt like I'd been whisked away by Mr. Darcy himself, and it felt charming and romantic. But I wasn't letting it go to my head. This was still my job, even though I was crashing on a bed in the next room over while trying to organize a half-dozen events.

"I have to survive, Kev." I frowned at him and finally found the list I was looking for. "Mike took the company name, all my directories, all my hopes. I need something to help bring in money, and when faced with the choice of an uncertain future with a mountain of marketing expenses I couldn't afford or this offer where I have to branch out a little, it was a no-brainer."

Kevin's eyes rolled again and I wondered if he'd sprain a ligament. He had no clue what it was like to struggle. He'd been born with a silver spoon in his mouth, which made him the perfect right-hand man because I'd done wedding plans for at least ten of his close friends. Now they were all married, though, and no one was knocking down my door for wedding planners. I had to branch out. There was no other way.

"Okay, but when you fail because you're not into this?" His eyes narrowed at me, and I was insulted at the fact that he wasn't even considering my feelings or the situation. That made me feel like he didn't believe in me.

"I'm doing this with or without you, buddy. I just thought you'd get on board." The day was wearing on me, and I was getting hungry. James and I had been having dinner together in the evenings because as a guest he felt it improper to let me starve. I didn't mind his invitations, which came every evening about this time for the past few days. It was nice to have another person to talk to.

"I just think you're wasting your time. You should be fighting Mike for the company, not changing your entire brand." Kevin stood and followed me to the door. I shut the lights off and walked out, and he stepped into the hallway behind me and didn't let up. "Mike doesn't deserve all that. You built it with your hard work, and it might've been his idea, but he has no clue how to do what you do. You should get the name and credentials."

While I appreciated what he was saying and fully agreed, I just didn't want to fight anymore. I'd done enough of that with Mike for the past nine months. I wanted something new, a change that would give my life meaning and purpose again.

"I appreciate your opinion, but I have to find my own way, Kevin." I wrapped my arms around his bicep and leaned my head on his shoulder the way I did when I wanted him to understand I meant no offense, but he was clearly offended. He pulled away and scowled at me. I was sad, but what could I do? We just didn't see eye to eye.

"Okay, but I'd just think your friends' opinions would mean more to you than some dumb client." We continued walking in silence, and I felt like speaking my mind, but I didn't. I didn't want to argue.

"Oh, Ms. Hart... And...?" James walked out of his office as we passed on the way to the front door. Kevin immediately tensed, and I felt like scolding him. James was a sweet man with great advice, and he believed in me. I wished my own friend would believe in me like that.

"This is Kevin," I told him, and Kevin shook his hand but didn't look happy about it.

"Hello, Kevin. I'm James Carver. Ivy is working for me." He glanced at me when Kevin said nothing and then he continued. "Would you two like to join me for dinner? I hear we're having delicious savory roast and vegetables tonight." Just the mere mention of the food made my stomach grumble. I was starving. All I had for lunch were an apple and a few carrot sticks. I was too busy to go out and get something else.

"I'd love that, thank you," I said and smiled at him.

Kevin's nostrils flared and he sighed. "I have plans, thank you. Another time. See you tomorrow, Ivy."

Both of us watched Kevin walk away, and I couldn't help but wish he'd have just been cordial. I hated that my client had to witness his being immature, but James turned to me with a smile and extended his elbow.

"Shall we?" he asked, and I smiled at him. I put my hand around his arm and heard the door click shut behind us as we headed toward the kitchen.

Kevin would get over himself soon enough. He was always a little hot headed, but he'd come around. If not, we'd just bicker until he saw me being successful, then he'd admit I hadn't made such a horrible decision after all.

Until then, I had a job to do and dinner to eat. And I was looking forward to spending more time with Mr. Carver. He had a way of building me up that I appreciated, and I was craving it after that interaction with Kevin.

5

JAMES

It was odd the way Ivy's friend jetted out the door after my invitation for dinner, but they seemed tense when I walked out of my office and startled them. I chalked it up to their having a spat and nothing more and escorted her to the dining room.

The smell of roast and vegetables wafted through the air to greet us, and Marna was already setting the table. She smiled as we walked in and said, "Good evening, Mr. Carver, Ms. Hart." Her polite nod was always accompanied by that same smile. Marna seemed to never miss a beat, though I knew she was just as human as the rest of us.

"Thank you for the meal, Marna. You can go home now. I'll make sure Ms. Hart is well cared for." I pulled out Ivy's chair for her as my maid thanked me for the dismissal. She headed back into the kitchen, and I sat at the head of the table to Ivy's left.

"Wow, this smells so yummy." Her eyes grew wide as she looked down at her plate full of food. It was normal for me to eat homecooked food daily, and I was pleased that Ivy was enjoying it too.

"I assure you, it is." My cloth napkin snapped in the air as I shook it out and draped it over my knee. "How are things going with the plans?" I asked Ivy, and she settled in to eat and chat with me.

We'd been dining together each evening. As my guest, I found it only fitting to invite Ms. Hart to enjoy a meal. Besides, I hated eating alone, and it was a great opportunity for us to stay up to date on all the festivities. Ivy had a lot of irons in the fire, but she seemed well on top of things.

"I am finishing the plans for Thanksgiving. It's a huge task to take on. I'm shocked your wife was able to manage it on her own." Her comment made me tense, but I tried not to let it show.

Thinking about Barbra was no longer a pleasant thing. I used to sit and think about her while I worked and wonder what she was doing. I'd send her a message or have a quick call. We talked a lot more in the beginning, but the busyness of life and my work just got in the way and we stopped thinking of each other as much.

"Yes, well she had my entire staff too," I said, but it came out more like a grumble.

"Gosh... I'm sorry." Ivy's head dropped, and I felt bad for discouraging her. It was all so fresh to me, and there was no way she could have known I'd react poorly to that, but her head popped back up. She smiled and continued. "I think you'll love the seating charts this year, and I have the cutest little cornucopias coming from Canada. Oh, and the Riesling will be sweet—straight from Germany. I think you're going to love it."

I chuckled as I took a bite of roast and admired her sass. She seemed to have it all together. When she started talking about Christmas and how my entire home would be transformed into a winter wonderland complete with snowed windows and Elf on the Shelf, I paused my eating to admire again how she made it all seem so easy. Every year, Barbra complained about the modest things she did to prepare our home for the holidays. Ivy seemed to love it.

"And the Valentine's gala?" I asked her. This one was what I was nervous about. I had dumped so much money into securing the venue and the caterer, not to mention the invitations which had to be completely redone now. My friends would be shocked to hear I was not only not renewing my vows, but in fact, a divorce was underway or would even be final by then. I wanted lots of wine on tap for all those romantics to drown their sorrows in.

"Well, I have a bit of time. I've been focusing on the events that are closer, but I'm thinking we transform the entire thing into a masquerade. What do you think? We'll have a photo booth with a photographer to do portraits, and everyone will wear masks, just like in Victorian France." Ivy's eyes sparkled as she spoke, and I could tell she was really getting into this.

"You're not just a wedding planner, Ms. Hart," I told her, pointing my empty fork at her. "You seem to be really enjoying yourself."

She sipped her wine nervously, and I watched her cheeks flush pink. It was adorable. In fact, she was gorgeous when that happened. Her shy embarrassment at taking a compliment was a turn-on for me. It made me want to lavish her in more praise just to see her blush again.

"And you handle the stress of it all so well. How do you do that? Barbra used to hate…" I realized my fumble before it was out of my mouth, but I couldn't stop it.

Ivy's expression sobered to one of compassion, and she reached out and touched my hand softly. "It's okay. You can talk about her if you need to. I know the holidays will be rough for you. I don't want you to think I'm trying to purposefully outdo her or anything." Her fingers lingered on my hand, and I noticed how she looked into my eyes with such empathy.

"It's okay." I smiled curtly and sucked in a breath, but I ended up talking despite my reservation about it. "Barbra and I just weren't going to be able to make it work. We lost that spark a long time ago and I never could rekindle it."

She finished her glass of wine, and I refilled it for her, then topped mine off too. Things were quiet for a few minutes as I watched her take a few bites, then she looked up at me and asked, "What went wrong?" Her honest question sounded more like a wish for hope and understanding, not nosiness or prying. I could see the look in her eye that begged an answer, as if she herself wanted to believe in love again.

"Well, we were good in the beginning, but somewhere along the line, I just stopped giving her as much attention as she wanted. I was busy working and trying to build my tech firm. She wanted more, so she found someone to give her attention and—"

"Oh, God, she cheated on you?" Ivy brought a hand to her lips and covered her mouth as I nodded slowly and then dropped my head.

"I thought she was happy doing her yoga classes and scrapbooking clubs. I didn't realize she needed more time with me than just evenings and weekends. I found her with him and then..." I stopped. She didn't need those details. "Anyway, I tried my hardest to forgive her and look past it, accept my own part in the blame and move on, but she was done."

Ivy stared down at her plate as she set her fork on the table and her shoulders drooped. "I feel like that's me too. I mean..." Her eyes rose to meet mine and she said, "Mike was just domineering from the beginning. I wished he'd have let me be a bit more independent like you were with your wife, but he just controlled everything. I need to be my own person and have the ability to make choices for myself. He just never saw that."

For a moment, we held each other's gaze, and it felt like we were on the same wavelength. Ivy had just been through more than a bad breakup. Maybe she wasn't with this Mike guy as long as I had been with Barbra, but they shared a business venture and I knew that was hell to untangle.

"I'm certain you deserved it. Unfortunately, what I gave Barbra wasn't to her liking and she made it known."

Ivy rubbed her eyes and then smiled at me sadly. "I always thought love was what you give to someone, not what they give to you. I mean, sure, there's an aspect to someone treating you well in return, but love is free. Or it should be. Love should be what you give, not what you expect. I don't think I ever loved Mike." Her frown as she looked back down at her half-eaten food told me all I needed to know.

I sighed and draped my napkin over my empty plate and stood. "I should escort you to your room."

"Ah, a magical after dinner walk to cure all that ails me." She took my hand and rose, letting the napkin draped over her knee fall to the ground. It was then that I knew she was feeling the effects of the alcohol, and I chuckled at her comment.

"If I had that magical touch, I would definitely cure any ails you have." My chest fluttered as she wrapped both arms around my bicep and rested her head on my shoulder. It'd been a long time since a woman had touched me like this. More than a year, in fact. Barbra was never the clingy type physically, either.

"I would definitely let you touch me," Ivy said, and she snickered and then started laughing so hard she snorted.

I was flattered that she, being so much younger than me, was flirting with me like this, but I didn't put a whole lot of stock into what any drunk person said to me. Even if it was a gorgeous younger woman making a pass at me in my own home after a dinner that got intimate.

"Let's get you to bed," I told her, patting her hand, and she looked up at me dreamily.

"James," she said, and then she paused speaking, though we continued to move through the house toward her bedroom.

"Yes, Ms. Hart?" My hand remained wrapped around hers on my arm, and the slight haze of alcohol in her eyes cleared.

"Why don't you call me Ivy? Everyone calls me Ivy." We stopped outside her door, and I opened it for her and flipped on the light.

"Goodnight, Ms. Hart," I said softly.

I got her into her room and shut the door, then retreated to my room and shed my clothing before climbing into bed. As I let the stress of the day fade out of my body and sleep crawl closer, I thought about what Ivy said at dinner. *Love is free.*

Love should have been what I gave Barbra our whole marriage, championing her and being there for her. But I had spent so much time nurturing my dreams and not her. What she did was definitely wrong, but I didn't really set her up for success because I never truly loved her. I liked how she made me feel. Maybe I never loved her at all, not even a little.

That was something I needed to learn to do if I was ever going to be successful in a future relationship. And I had Ivy to thank for teaching me that.

6

IVY

With the task of hosting a few different parties in this very same ballroom, I set out today to get every single measurement I could think of. The hotel staff were very helpful too, offering me step ladders and assisting me when needed. Kevin couldn't help me this afternoon since Mike needed him, and my sister Mimi, who often stepped in to help me, had other plans too.

I stood in the center of the ballroom imagining a large ball dangling from the center with a table beneath it covered in food. At its center, a chocolate fountain would be the highlight of the Valentine's gala, but for the company Christmas gathering next month, it would be the stage where the dais would be raised and Mr. Carver's podium would stand, where he would address his staff.

As I stepped back and closed my eyes to picture everything in my head, I heard a noise behind me. It startled me, and I pressed my hand to my chest and turned to see the hotel manager bringing a steaming cup of some sort of drink toward me.

"Ms. Hart, I thought you could use a cup of coffee." She glanced around the ballroom. I hadn't done much but take measurements and mark them down on my notebook, but she glanced down at me and smiled. "Is the space everything you thought it would be?"

I took the cup of coffee from her and nodded. It smelled heavenly, and it was exactly what I needed. "Actually, it's better than I thought. These high ceilings will be great for the lighting I plan to hang..." I thought about it for a second. "Do you have a scissor lift my team can use?" I used the word "team" as if I had a team. Right now it was just me and Kevin, though to pull this off, I really would have to hire a crew.

"Of course we do. Our maintenance team uses one to change lightbulbs." She looked up at the ceiling and frowned. "Like that one that's out. I'll have them ensure all of our lighting is working properly for you ASAP." Her soft smile returned as she looked back at my face. "Have you gotten all your measurements?" Her eyes flicked to my notebook, and I held it up.

"All written down right here."

"It's so refreshing to see that some people still respect paper and pencil." Her chuckle made me laugh too.

"Believe me, this is all going into my laptop when I get back to the Carver estate." I thought of James and dinner last week when I flirted with him. It was the last dinner I shared with him before he went out of town on a quick business trip. I felt like a fool, and I knew the only reason I flirted was because I'd been drinking. But he was a handsome man, and any woman in my position would have been tempted.

"Good, well I hope you are able to get everything you need. If you have any questions or need anything, just stop by the front desk." She smiled and bowed from the shoulders and backed away. I watched her walk across the ballroom in the opposite direction from which she'd come and thought about how attentive the staff was being. I knew my name didn't bring any prestige or attention, but dropping Mr. Carver's name seemed to make things happen.

The coffee was hot and my mind was still whirring with ideas. I set the cup and my notebook down and walked back to the center of the room, starting to completely rethink my idea. A chocolate fountain would be amazing, but what was more iconic at a masquerade ball than to have a dance? I twirled around and pressed my hands together over my chest and smiled. It was exactly what we needed. Though, this carpeted floor had to go.

I could have a wood floor installed over top of the carpet for dancing, and I could hire an orchestra to come and play live music. If I gave it a very vintage French Victorian feel, James's gala would be the talk of the town, and that was exactly what I needed—both for him and for me. This ball could very well be the thing that catapulted my new party planning business into success. I would meet and rub elbows with as many of his friends and associates as possible, and I was sure if I asked him, he'd put in a good word.

The grin that crept over my face couldn't be stopped. But when I heard someone clear their throat, I startled again. My heart raced as I turned thinking I'd see another member of hotel staff, but instead it was James. He stood in the doorway staring at me with a look of enjoyment.

"Mr. Carver..." I felt instantly ashamed and wondered if he'd seen me do that little spin of excitement. "What are you doing here?" I hadn't given him my itinerary, nor had I told him where I'd be. He was still out of town as of this morning when I left the house, so I was shocked to see him here.

"Ms. Hart," he said, nodding at me. His charming smile made me blush again. I hated that. Any time I felt even slightly attracted to him, my damn face lit up like Rudolph's nose. "I stopped by your workspace at the house and you weren't there. I hope you don't mind. I checked your schedule and saw you'd be here."

He walked into the ballroom and up to the table I was using as my makeshift desk. My coffee sat there with my notebook and a dozen or so scrawlings I'd have to change now that I decided to nix the chocolate fountain focal point and replace it with a dance floor.

"Of course not. Do you need something?" I asked, feeling nervous. My body felt like I'd drunk too much coffee when I'd barely had a sip. Being near him made me feel jittery. I shouldn't have been attracted to him, but there was no point in denying the truth. He was hot, and I liked that he gave me attention and praise. Maybe I was stupid for deceiving myself that it was personal and not just business, but I was on the rebound.

"I'm just checking in..." His eyes scanned the ballroom the same way the hotel manager's had moments ago. "I saw you dancing. Are you a good dancer?" His question made a lump form in my throat.

"Uh, that was more of a celebratory twirl because I got a great idea. I'm not a dancer." My cheeks burned hotter than the surface of the sun as I looked down at my notebook and tried to keep my eyes from catching his gaze. I thought he hadn't seen that. I felt so embarrassed.

"But there will be dancing, right?" he asked. "At the gala, I mean. We always have a few dances at my parties."

I wasn't sure if he was just saying that, but my shoulders tightened as I lifted my head. I was glad my brain had given me that ah-ha moment. "Of course. I was just envisioning a dance floor," I told him as he walked away.

James moved toward the center of the room where I'd done my spin, and he stood there looking down at his phone. I didn't know what he was doing, but he looked up at the ceiling then at me. "Right here? A dance floor?"

"Well, yes..." I fumbled for words as he looked back down at his phone as it started playing music. He turned it up, then slid it into his pocket and held his arm out toward me.

"Join me. I'm assuming you know how to dance if a man leads."

Nervous jitters washed down my body, and I pressed my lips into a line. He was asking me to dance with him now? As if testing out an imaginary dancefloor right here and now.

I walked toward him and took his hand, and he pulled me against his chest in one tug. One of my hands rested on his shoulder while he held the other in the air, and I was swept away. The music floated through the air, loud enough for us to hear but not loud enough to be heard outside the room, and he spun me around effortlessly. I barely had to do anything but keep in step with him.

James's eyes were locked on mine, and I couldn't look away, even as he spun and moved me. His body felt good against mine too. We gelled like seasoned partners who knew each other's steps so well they could do it blindfolded, and then he spoke.

"You know, I'll have a dance at each event that I will need a partner for. Since… well, you know. Since I'm single now, I would think any number of women would be able to fill that spot on my dance card, but I'm not really looking to be acquainted with anyone so soon." He looked thoughtful. "Would you, perhaps, mind being my dance partner those evenings? You know, just so I have someone to dance with."

I knew I had flirted with him openly that night, even asking him to touch me, but this was next-level. Both of us were stone-cold sober and we were in a ballroom dancing in each other's arms. It was romantic and poetic and I was an idiot, but I really wanted to say yes.

But I didn't. At least not at first.

"Mr. Carver—"

"James," he said, cutting me off.

"James, your wife just left you. I just got dumped. I think…" I bit my lip and tried so hard to pull my eyes away, but I couldn't.

"One dance, each night. You'll be there anyway to make sure things go smoothly, right?" He wasn't looking hopeful. He was staring at me like I was his prey, and I wanted so badly to be devoured.

"Yes."

"Yes, you'll be there or yes, you'll dance with me?" Now he was smirking, looking satisfied that he'd trapped me.

I almost grumbled, but I held it back. A hot, wealthy man was asking me to dance with him at his party. What was wrong with me?

"Of course I will." I smiled, and as soon as the words were out of my mouth, he stepped back and bowed at the waist, then straightened.

"Good day, Ms. Hart. I'll see you for dinner."

James walked away with his chin held high and the music still lofting through the air, and I swooned at how romantic he was. My God, I'd have given anything for him to have been the man of my dreams, but that was all he could be. He was just a dream. A man that wealthy and esteemed—not to mention that much older than me—would never actually look my way.

If James Carver wanted something from me, it was simply to plan his parties and make him look good, nothing more. I had to keep my head out of the clouds or I was going to get my heart broken.

7

JAMES

I walked out of the ballroom and past the hotel's front desk feeling confident. After that conversation with Ivy at my dinner table, I felt like a huge weight had been lifted off my shoulders. For a long time, the idea of divorce didn't feel like freedom. It felt like a stain on my life that I'd never be able to remove because it marked me as a failure. I'd been raised to believe the institution of marriage was a once and you're done thing. That Barbra was it for me.

But along came Ivy Hart to dismantle everything I'd ever thought in just a few words. She'd said love should be free, and that made me rethink everything I thought about love. I'd spent the past five days away from my home out of town, and each night as I dined alone and lay in my bed contemplating life, I thought about those words.

I had never once truly loved Barbra. I did care about things, and when she was ill, I cared for her. But my goals and hopes for my own life always took precedence. I was selfish, though I never thought of it like that. I assumed when my business was established well enough, my focus would turn toward a family, but as Ivy spoke about what real love looked like, I realized I'd never experienced it—not as a giver or a receiver.

Barbra never loved me, either. She wasn't the doting, supportive wife who catered to my needs and encouraged me. She was every bit as selfish, constantly nagging me to change and be better. She always harped on me to do this or do that, and honestly, not having that pressure on my shoulders for the past few weeks had been refreshing to me. It was like I could breathe again, like an obligation I wasn't enjoying had been removed from my list of priorities and I was free.

I climbed into my limo and shut the door, and my driver looked at me through my reflection in the rearview mirror. His eyes studied me for a second and finally, I gave him orders.

"To the office now, please." He nodded and took off, and I looked down at my phone.

Ivy Hart had helped me break through a barrier I doubted I'd have ever torn down myself, mostly because I'd have stayed stuck in a mentality that wasn't healthy. I knew if the right person came along, my heart would devote itself fully to that person. There wouldn't be any effort needed or involved. I'd want to make them happy and make their dreams come true. And Barbra just hadn't been that.

I felt so grateful to have met Ms. Hart, and now after hearing what she'd been going through the past few months, how she needed to rebuild and rebrand her business to survive, I wanted to help her. I wasn't going to just dump millions on her lap and tell her a cold "Thanks." I wanted to do something better for her. Something that would make a strong impact on her that would last a lifetime, the way she'd made an impact on me.

Smiling, I opened my phone and navigated to the website where my RSVP's for all of my gatherings were being collected. I thumbed through the list of people who said they'd come and I started making a few mental notes of the men and women I'd want to introduce her to. I knew some very social people who would definitely have parties and gatherings of their own that Ivy would be perfect for, and I wanted to make sure I didn't let a single opportunity slip by me where I could put in a good word or make an introduction.

Then I happened upon a few single men who recently came into my radar, good men who were responsible and level-headed. I knew they weren't necessarily looking for a partner, but then neither was Ms. Hart at the moment. Still, it never hurt to introduce her to them. She might very well hit it off with one of them and find the love of her life, because a woman with a heart of gold like hers deserved a wonderful man to love her.

I might've been too old or out of touch for someone her age, but that didn't mean I couldn't still support her and help her. If by introducing her to a few people, I put wind in her sails, then I would do it. I was making the decision right here and now to show her that there were still really great men in the world who would treat her better than her former partner, and they would help her chase her dreams. And it was a good feeling.

8

IVY

Anger radiated off me in what I was certain were visible waves, the way heat wafts upward off hot concrete in the summer. I was livid. My phone was pressed to my ear in a grip so tight I thought I'd bend the thing in half.

"No, Mike. You don't get everything. I need that van. This is ridiculous. How am I supposed to get everything organized and transported across town without a vehicle? It's my name on that lease too. You can't do this."

The delivery van Mike and I purchased as our primary vehicle was actually owned by the company, half of which was mine. When we bought it, he couldn't qualify for it on his own, so I had to co-sign and I'd done that with the assumption that we'd end up being married and have two-point-three children, a dog, and a white picket fence around our yard. He clearly didn't agree with that dream.

"I don't know what to tell you, Ivy. The van literally has *Ever After Events'* written right on the side of it. It's mine because you left me. I didn't leave you." I was so angry I could scream at him, and I was raising my voice but not to that level yet.

"I chose that name. That business is half mine and you know it. I am coming to get the van. I need it today." I huffed and felt tears welling up in my eyes.

Why did I always have to cry? Why, when I got angry, were tears my go-to response? I couldn't just be a normal person and shout at someone to give them a piece of my mind. I had to break down like a fucking baby and bawl.

"I'm sorry, but the van is in use. Jess has it out on deliveries all day, and when this whole thing is sorted, I'm petitioning the court to have your name removed from the lease and the registration. You can't just walk out on our company and think you get to take half. If you want your half, you should've stayed."

I scream-growled and stomped my foot in rage, but I knew it would do no good. Mike had never been the sort of person to be reasoned with. He knew what he wanted and he took it, and when I finally got up the nerve to walk out, he took that as my cue that I wasn't interested in my company either. It was my blood, sweat, and tears. He just ran the back end. I did the hard work. Now none of it was mine, not even the name.

"Fine... You're right. I didn't want you, and I don't want your stupid company, or your name, or the van either. Have it." The first tear streaked down my cheek, and I blinked a few more back, but I knew I'd lost. There wasn't any point in fighting him when he was being like this. I learned that a long time ago. Mike always got what he wanted when he wanted it.

"I'm glad you see it my way. Have a good day, Ivy." Mike hung up with his smug, asshole tone, and I threw my phone across the room. It landed on the pillows and bounced back onto the mattress. I hadn't made the bed, and it slid under the blanket where I couldn't see it as I covered my face with my hands.

It was just like him to leave me stranded. I had to pick up the centerpieces and floral arrangements for Mr. Carver's thanksgiving party this afternoon. We were just a few days out and the shop I chose didn't do deliveries. It was the only place that could get me the right shades, the ones Kevin insisted would be hard to source, but I went with it. Now I was regretting that choice and wishing I'd have listened to Kevin, who was usually right.

"Everything okay?" I heard, and I turned around to see James standing in my bedroom doorway. I felt a bit embarrassed that the place was a bit disorganized and messy. I didn't let Marna come in here, mostly because I didn't like the idea of making someone else clean up after me when I was quite capable of it myself. I cringed and sighed as I wiped tears off my cheeks.

"Uh, just had an argument with Mike." I sniffled, and James stepped forward and handed me his monogrammed handkerchief. It was so pretty with royal blue thread embroidered into the white cotton. I didn't want to mess it up. I tried to hand it back, but he pushed it toward me again. So I wiped my eyes and blew my nose on it.

"Are you okay?" he asked again, and this time, I felt like he meant it. Like he wanted to make sure I was doing alright emotionally.

"I think I'm okay. I'm just left with a tricky situation." My shoulders sagged, and I backed up to the bed and sat down. It was so embarrassing, yet again, that I was having to ask someone to help me. This wasn't James's problem, though the reason I needed the van was for his party. I could probably rent a van with the money he paid me, but I really didn't want to dip into the budget for that considering in February when this was all said and done, I needed money to find a place to rent.

"Well, I just happen to be excellent at ironing out tricky situations." He smiled and stepped farther into the room. "What is the issue?" James folded his hands and let them hang in front of him, and I sighed and told him about the argument and the problem with the flowers and centerpieces. Even his largest limo wouldn't be enough. I didn't know how to make it happen without a van, and I wasn't asking him to rent one for me.

James turned and held out his elbow toward me, and I looked up at him confused. "Come," he said, and I stood and let my fingers curl around his bicep.

He led me out the front door toward his limo, and I thought of my phone lying on my bed, which made me panic for a minute. But the only person I'd miss hearing from if they called would be my mother or my sister. I was upset with Kevin for ditching me, and Mike could go to hell. Anyone else could leave a message.

James had his driver take us to the flower shop. We talked about the party and who would all be there. Tomorrow's dinner was being catered by Renard's out of Green Bay—so pricey, but it was what he wanted. They would be at the house to set up later this evening and get things rolling. I had to coordinate lighting and tables and music. This was the last thing I needed, but James's willingness to help made me feel more confident.

"Here we are," he said as the limo came to a stop. He climbed out first and offered me his hand. As we strolled into the store, people's heads turned. He wasn't exactly famous, but the two-thousand-dollar suit he wore spoke volumes. A woman standing behind the counter smiled and made her way over toward us with a shuffle-step, and I figured she thought she was going to make a huge sale today. She was, but she already knew about my order.

"Hi there, how can I help you?" Her hand shot out toward James's and she ignored me completely. I assumed it was because he was dressed to the nines, closer to her age than mine, and very good-looking. She probably thought I was his daughter.

"Well, Ms. ...?" James waited, and the woman filled in the blanks.

"Mrs. Harper," she said with a smile and a few swipes of her eyelashes. Gross.

"Mrs. Harper, this is Ms. Ivy Hart. She's planning a party for me and she placed an order with you a few days ago for some floral arrangements and such. We'd like to see if you can deliver them." James had such a commanding presence, the woman nearly wilted. She looked faint.

"Well, Mr. Carver, I'm sure you understand that we don't have a van for deliveries and—"

"How much?" he asked, and I had to hide a grin behind my hand. She'd made an educated guess about this being Mr. Carver after I'd told her for whom I was ordering the arrangements. Now she was seeing exactly why that name carried power. She had fought me tooth and nail about getting them done on time to begin with.

Mrs. Harper blanched and shook her head apologetically. "I'm sure you understand—"

"How much?" he repeated, more firmly. And she sucked in a breath and looked around.

"Sir, we don't have a van." Her eyebrows rose and she looked as if she might start to cry at any moment.

"Go right now, research whatever van it is you want, and come back and tell me how much to make the delivery happen before eight a.m. tomorrow morning, and I'll have the funds transferred." He pointed at the counter, and this time, it was his eyebrows that rose in a very dominant and expectant expression.

"Well, sir... I... well..." She huffed and sighed and glanced at me before turning around and walking to the counter.

When she vanished into a back office, James turned to me and smirked. "Money talks," he said, scrunching his nose.

"It's gonna cost you eighty grand to have a thousand dollars' worth of floral arrangements and cornucopias delivered." I laughed, and he shrugged.

"Totally worth it to see the look on her face." His eyebrows wagged, and he reached to pick up a flower from a nearby vase. It was a single mum, and it was beautiful. He handed it to me, and I, like an idiot, dropped it. My hands were shaking. He was being so sweet.

"God, I'm so sorry," I blurted out as I bent to retrieve it, but he bent at the same time and our heads smacked together hard.

I saw stars for a second as I righted myself and leaned on a display table to keep my balance. James picked up the flower and stepped closer to me so that I was cocooned in his cologne. I'd have sworn it made me drunk on him, but that was probably the knock to the head.

"I'm so sorry," I said again, and he smiled.

His hand rose up to my face, cupping my cheek. He brushed his thumb over what I could only assume was a red spot on my forehead, and then his eyes dropped to mine. "Not a mark…" he whispered, then his eyes dropped to my lips.

They lingered there, watching as I bit my lip. His thumb pressed against it, pulling it out from between my teeth. Then he brushed it over my bottom lip a few times as he said, "You know, you're extremely beautiful when you smile."

"I…" I started to say, feeling consumed with him. He was so close, his eyes bouncing between my eyes and my lips, and I swore he was leaning in.

Then the bell over the door behind him chimed and I stepped back as I heard Kevin's voice. "Have no fear, Kevin is here!" he sang out, and I looked away as James's hand left my face. "Mike is a douche, but I got the van. Jess didn't need it…" He glanced at James, then at me, then back to James. "I have the van."

"Um, yes. Thank you, Kevin." I knew he knew what was happening based on the look on his face, and I knew I'd have to answer for that. I just hoped he had tact.

"Thank you, Kevin," James said, extending his hand. Kevin shook it but narrowed his eyes at us both. "Ivy, I guess you're all set here. I'll see you this evening," he said, and he walked out of the store. I watched him until he walked out of my line of sight, and then I turned to Kevin, ready to hear his lecture.

James Freaking Carver almost kissed me. Oh, my God. What was happening?

9

JAMES

My reflection in the mirror stared back at me as I tied my tie and prepared for my workday. The greys at my temple were growing in thicker, and my beard was seeing a few more silvers appear too, but I only started really noticing them in the past month when it occurred to me that I wasn't growing old alongside the woman who had promised to do that with me.

This morning, she wasn't even the woman on my mind anymore. It was funny to me how for years I spent every waking second thinking of her. Then I spent my time thinking of my company. Then for a short time, the obsession with all things Barbra returned but in a very traumatic way, a way I'd like to forget never happened.

Now my thoughts were on Ms. Ivy Hart and her incredible smile. The look on her face—of awe and admiration—when I told that florist to name her price for delivery was priceless. She was adorable, and I found myself smitten, especially when we bumped heads and I checked to make sure she was alright. I'd have kissed her too, if her friend wouldn't have come in. I was poised to do it. My lips tingled to feel hers against them and my fingers itched to curl through her hair and pull her into me.

Even now as I finished my double Windsor, a smile crept across my lips. Her reaction was what made me fully believe that if I had actually kissed her, she'd have kissed me back. Her hand fluttered up to her face, fingers dancing over her lip as I backed away and smiled at her. The friend seemed to have read the situation, but I ducked out gracefully.

Ms. Hart and I were leagues apart in almost every way. I had so much money I could burn it in my fireplace as warmth for my home in winter. I'd picked up over the past several weeks in our conversations that she was looking for a place to live. My firm dealt in expensive microchips that went into luxury electric vehicles and other sorts of things while she was a party planner tasked with crafting luxury experiences in her own way.

And the fact that I was forty-five and she was less than thirty didn't escape me. I wasn't quite old enough to be her father, but I was from a different generation. We grew up throwing sticks in the river and building forts in the trees. She grew up with an iPad in her hand texting her best friends on the internet. I wasn't even sure what women her age liked or enjoyed, and here I was with designs for her.

The wind left my sails at the thought, and I smoothed my hand back over my hair. The chemistry between us was real, but chemistry isn't the only thing needed for a relationship. Whatever I had with Barbra had started much the same way, but we never found our groove, never had much in common upon which to build something lasting. My admiration for Ms. Hart had to be harnessed and caged or I'd end up with the same sort of failure, and she didn't deserve that.

I left my bedroom dressed for my important meetings this morning and ready to leave, but I headed down to the kitchen to get a cup of coffee before I headed out. It was early, much earlier than a normal day, but the meetings couldn't wait. When I popped through the kitchen door, Marna wasn't even here preparing breakfast for Ms. Hart yet, though I'd told her not to worry about me this morning.

What I did see was a sight that made my body warm to a sizzling temperature and my dick start to swell. Ms. Hart stood by the back door that led out to the veranda with one foot lifted behind herself and held there by an outstretched arm. She looked graceful and poised. She had earbuds in her ears, and her body shimmered with sweat. She wore a matching green sports bra and spandex, and her hair was tied up in a ponytail.

I had to stop myself from drooling as I took her in. The sight of her made any rational thought fly right out of my head, and I completely forgot every reason that it wouldn't work between us. In that moment, all I knew was that I was a man with a sex drive and she was a stunning woman with curves like a backroad I wanted to cruise all day.

"Oh, Mr. Carver..." She put her foot down and smiled, then turned and removed her earbuds. "I didn't see you there. I was just about to step outside to cool down after my run."

Okay, so I actually was drooling a little. Even soaked in sweat, she was the most gorgeous creature on the planet.

"I didn't mean to interrupt," I told her as I took a few more steps into the kitchen, forgetting why I even came in here. "And I asked you to call me James."

"Well I asked you to call me Ivy," she said with a smile as she curled a stray strand of hair around her ear.

"Indeed, you did..." I hovered halfway between the door and the island, and she remained across the island by the exterior door. It seemed, however, like there was an ocean between us, and I wanted to close that gap, but I didn't want to seem too forward. The gap wasn't just the kitchen island topped in marble. It was an entire universe of differences I'd have to account for.

"Ms. Hart, do you have plans for dinner tomorrow evening?" I always asked her to dinner. That was nothing special, but I felt like doing something out of the ordinary, and I wanted her to know it was out of the ordinary. The first Friday of December was no special day except that I hoped it would be a day where I could get to know her better and find out just how different or similar we were.

"Not really. I planned to have dinner here." She bobbed one shoulder up and down, and her ponytail swayed and the tiniest dimple appeared on her cheek.

"Good," I said, now feeling more confident. "I have plans this evening, but I want you to clear your schedule for tomorrow. Be here at one and be ready for a transformation. I'll pick you up at six. I'm taking you to dinner."

"James, I..." She looked like she was going to refuse my invitation, so I cut her off.

"Please, Ivy?" I said, and her eyebrows rose. I much preferred calling her Ms. Hart. The way it rolled off my tongue felt sophisticated and classy. But it worked like a charm.

"Dinner, tomorrow at six. I'll be ready." Her posture relaxed, and she smiled as she slid her earbuds back into her ears and I backed out of the room.

Only when I had climbed into my limo and shut the door did I realize that I hadn't picked up my coffee, but I had picked up something even better. My date for tomorrow evening might not even realize she was on a date until I made that part obvious, but I hoped she wouldn't react negatively when she found out that I considered it one. I hoped her reaction would be more like the one she gave me as my thumb slid over her bottom lip as I prepared to kiss her.

I settled in for my commute to work and took out my phone. This called for a special touch. I figured Ivy would feel out of place if I took her to a fancy restaurant while wearing my Armani suit and Rolex. The way she dressed was fine by any standards, and I didn't look down on her simple suits and dresses, but I wanted her to feel like a princess, so I called my friend Genevieve and asked a favor.

"Hello? Yes, James." She sounded happy to hear from me, which meant Barbra probably hadn't shared the news to her yet.

"Gen," I said, "so good to hear your voice."

"All the same to you, dear. What can I do for you?"

"Gen, I need a huge favor..." I cringed a little inwardly when I realized what I was doing. Genevieve was still friends with Barbra, and word would get out that I was having another woman styled, and I wasn't sure what to think of that so far before my Valentine's gala where I'd make the announcement that Barbra and I were separating. My lawyer had already gotten annulment paperwork from Barbra's lawyer, so it wasn't like she was changing her mind. But so soon after she officially left my house felt like I was the cheater, not her. Still, it was her choice and this could be chalked up to a business meeting. Ivy, after all, did work for me.

"Of course, anything for you, dear."

The car bumped over the road as I explained to Genevieve what I expected. I wanted the full workup for Ivy, whatever she'd do for Barbra when we had an event. I told her Ivy worked for me and was staying at my home and for this particular business meeting, we were putting on the Ritz. She seemed to understand my instructions and seemed thankful that I'd thought of her.

"You know, dear, people are talking..." Genevieve said, and I found my mood souring slightly. I knew people would talk and I didn't care as long as I didn't have to hear about it.

"I'm sure they're saying this year's Christmas event will be the biggest yet. I'll see you there, right?" My command of the conversation steered it away from gossip and toward better things, and I heard the shift of emotion in Genevieve's tone as she agreed.

"Yes, yes. I'll be there with bells on. Literally," she said, chuckling. "My dress will have jingle bells!"

"Fantastic. Just don't expect to sit on Santa's lap. I heard he's taken." My joke hit its mark, and I finished the conversation before I got waylaid into answering twenty questions. "See you then, Gen. And just send me the bill."

"Tootles, James. Have a good day."

I hung up and let the storm clouds gather. It was fascinating to me how my mood could go from light and happy to angry and brooding in just a few moments' time. Barbra had every right to talk about what was going on in our relationship because it was directly concerning her and her mental state. I just wished she'd keep it to herself until I had time to fully process it and understand my own feelings. One minute I was angry, the next happy, and all over the women in my life.

My smile returned as I looked out the tinted window at passing cars on the road. The women in my life... Or woman, I should say. Ivy Hart, the woman in my life. I liked the sound of that.

I hoped she might like the sound of it too.

10

IVY

"Ms. Hart," I heard, and I looked up from my desk where I was sketching a design for the backdrop for the Valentine's gala photo booth. It was Marna, and she had a surprised look on her face. "Ms. Hart, Ms. Genevieve Porter is here to see you. Were you expecting her?"

The name didn't sound familiar at all, though why would it? And why would a strange woman come looking for me, anyway? But James did ask me to keep my afternoon clear and be ready, so I assumed this was part of his plan.

"I'm not sure," I said standing. "Show me to her, please." I smoothed my hands down the front of my skirt suit. I chose red today because I always thought it made me look good. The color was good for my complexion and suited my hair color too. And when James asked me to dinner and finally called me by my first name, how could I resist? I wanted to look my best, and this was it—though I was several hours early and very nervous.

Marna led me down the hall to another room I'd never been in, but the instant I walked in, I knew it was James's bedroom. His cologne sat on the dresser next to a pair of socks and a set of cufflinks. The whole room smelled wonderful just like him, but most distinctly, above the fireplace in the corner hung a hand-painted portrait of him and a beautiful woman. It was the same woman I'd seen storming down his driveway the day I first came here.

But what was most surprising was the woman standing next to his bed. She wore a gorgeous shimmery gown that reached to her ankles, and her light brown hair was curled and swept up on top of her head with picks and pins. She smiled, and her bright red lipstick caught my eye. She was stunning to look at and even her voice sounded like a melody when she spoke. I wondered if all of James's friends were this fancy.

"Ms. Hart, welcome..." She swept her hand around the room and gestured at two tall dress racks full of garment bags. There were boxes of shoes piled on the shelf below each rack of dresses, and she had another whole rolling set of drawers made of metal with a handle on top and a padlock keeping it secure.

"Hello," I said, feeling confused. "Ms. ...?"

"Genevieve, dear. Just Genevieve. James sent me, and here I am, and you are about to be transformed. Now... go on, start looking." She held her hand out toward the dress racks, and I stood there stunned speechless. What the heck was going on? I looked at Marna, who offered a confused and sympathetic expression as the woman chased her out. "Go on, Marna, get going. Ms. Hart and I have work to do."

Genevieve was spry for someone her age, at least fifty unless she looked as good for her age as she looked in general. She chased the maid out of the room, and when she shut the door and turned around, she moved swiftly toward me. With her hand in the small of my back, she ushered me toward the dress racks and started sifting through garment bags on her own. I had no idea what was even going on.

"Um, Ms. Porter, I'm sort of confused." I held a bag she shoved into my arms and then another and finally, after the third one, she smiled and turned her attention on me.

"Ms. Hart, James hired me to transform you. He said you have a business meeting this evening and he needs you looking absolutely smashing." Her eyes swept down my body to my feet and back up to my face. "And by the looks of it, you need my help."

I tried not to take offense to her statement, but it was sort of rude. "What help, exactly?" I thought I looked fine, though my heart was a little discouraged by the fact that she called this a business meeting. Was that why he asked me out? I was sort of hoping it was a date, but then he was so much older than me and so frickin' rich. I knew I was stupid for getting my hopes up.

"I'm a stylist, dear. Sullivan, Borcher, Malone... Where do you think they get their fashion sense?" Now her attitude was really showing. Ms. Genevieve Porter was a drama queen and a diva. "Go on. Take one of them and go into the bathroom and put it on..." She stared at me and swatted at me to shoo me away.

I frowned, but I picked one of the garment bags and laid the other two over the foot of James's bed and walked toward his bathroom. I thought my suit was nice enough, but this woman insisted I needed her "help" so I just let her herd me. I stepped into the bathroom and shut the door and hung the hanger for the garment bag on the hook on the back of the door.

James's bathroom was neat and tidy. He had a razor by the sink, a bar of soap as I'd expect, and his toothbrush. I smiled when I saw he squeezed the toothpaste in the middle just like me. Mike would've hated that. And when I spotted a T-shirt in the laundry hamper, I picked it up and breathed him in. It smelled like his cologne and musk, and I had to stop and enjoy that scent for a second.

Then Genevieve knocked and said, "I don't hear movement. Are you changing? We have a lot to do, honey."

"I'm changing," I grumbled and breathed in the scent of his T-shirt one more time before dropping it back into his hamper and beginning to undress. The whole idea of having to change myself for some man to accept me seemed ludicrous, and I was actually borderline on going to dinner now. If James Carver couldn't accept me the way I was, maybe he was a little too much like Mike, and maybe I didn't really like him as much as I thought I did.

I folded my clothes and set them to the side on the counter, then unzipped the bag. It was a stunning, sleeveless red gown with sparkling beads sewn into the fabric. It had a plunging neckline that would show off every bit of my chest and leave nothing to the imagination, and the back was entirely open. I'd be freezing.

"Uh, are you sure about this dress?" I asked, and I heard the stern woman huff from the other side of the door.

"Don't make me come in there," she scolded, and I carefully and quietly locked the door just to be sure I wasn't going to be walked in on.

Then I took the dress off the hanger and stepped into it. The zipper was only six inches long and stopped in the small of my back, but the front had wires in place to make sure my boobs stayed covered. I looked at myself in the mirror and cringed at the way my bra straps stuck out, but there was no way in hell I was going without one. I would just have to ask if she had something that would work for me. If James wanted me all spruced up, then I had to do it. Besides, I sort of felt like I was getting ready for high school prom, so I enjoyed it a little.

I stared at myself in the mirror for a few seconds and realized with the right bra, jewelry, and hairdo, I might just really enjoy wearing a pretty gown like this. Maybe James wasn't horrible for asking me to spiff up for him, but he would still get a piece of my mind if he thought this was what was acceptable. My clothes were just fine to me. I didn't want any man to try to change me.

The doorknob jiggled, and I sighed and turned to it and unlocked it and Genevieve burst in. "Well, that took long enough." I didn't know why she was being so rude to me, but I didn't care for it at all. She looked me over and clicked her tongue, but when I felt her icy fingers on my bra clasp, I gasped. She moved too quickly, undoing it and tugging it off me. The front of the dress shifted, and she threw my bra into the sink and nodded.

"There, that's better…" Her eyes narrowed and then her eyebrows rose and she tilted her head. Then she smiled.

All I could do was gawk. Even without makeup and jewelry, the dress looked really good on me. And I was surprised by how well the bodice covered my chest. I didn't actually feel all that uncomfortable. I admired myself in the mirror as she stalked around behind me and nodded.

"This is the one. No need to do anything else. Now… Get your ugly suit back on. We will do hair and nails before we dress." Genevieve grunted one last sound of approval and stormed out, slamming the door behind herself. I sighed and turned back to my reflection and smiled again.

Maybe it wouldn't be so bad after all.

For the next several hours, I got ushered from one room to another. Apparently, Genevieve had a whole team with her and they each had their own bedroom in the Carver estate to set up their stations. Francois cut and dyed my hair. I told him just a trim and he did a fantastic job. The way the highlights made my eyes pop was amazing. I felt like a princess.

Next was George who did my nails, French tips but in red, not white. He talked incessantly while he did them and I learned that Genevieve was Barbra's stylist—Barbra, who I was certain was James's ex-wife. No wonder Genevieve was nasty with me. She probably thought James had cheated on his wife with me.

Then I was moved on to Henry for a pedicure, Marie for a hairdo, and finally back to Genevieve and Sarah for my makeup. It was nearing five thirty when I finally slid back into that gown. When I accidentally let it drag on the ground, I got scolded. Genevieve made it clear that this dress was worth more than my entire life and I had to keep myself from rolling my eyes.

At precisely six p.m. on the dot, the front door opened and James walked in. Genevieve had me standing under the chandelier in the front entryway and the lighting was dim, but James's eyes widened and he didn't look away as he approached me carrying a velvet box in one hand.

"You look...." He didn't finish his sentence, and I could feel his stylist's eyes burning through my back. It felt very awkward to be in this situation, between his former wife's stylist and him when I wasn't even sure if he'd made it public knowledge that he was getting divorced yet. "Did they treat you well?" he asked in a low tone.

"Like a queen," I told him softly, and he smiled.

"For you..." James opened the velvet box, and I realized the one thing I was missing was in his hand.

A diamond necklace lay in the box stretched out, with a pair of diamond stud earrings to match. I smiled at them and then sighed.

"This is too much, Mr. Carver. It's so expensive." I tried not to push it away, but what if Genevieve was right and all of this cost more than my entire life? I didn't even own a car. It wouldn't be that big of a stretch.

"Wear them... For me." There was a sparkle in his eye that told me not to challenge him, so I took the earrings and put them on, then he lifted his chin at Genevieve and handed her the box. She put the necklace on me and backed away, and I felt complete.

"Shall we?" he asked, offering me his elbow, and without saying a word to his stylist, he ushered me out and into the limo.

Dinner started like normal except without food. During the drive, we recapped my plans for the few events I was in charge of during December, my plans and how things were progressing, and when we got to the restaurant, he got out and escorted me inside. The split second I saw the waiter's attire, I realized why James had done what he did. My modest business suit picked up at the local mall would've been laughed out of this place. Even the waiters' clothing cost more than my salary.

"James," I said nervously, feeling very out of place. Crystal chandeliers hung above each individual table. The gold in them mimicked the threads of gold that seemed to weave through the tile beneath our feet.

"Shh," he said, patting my hand, which was wrapped around his bicep. Which, by the way, was very firm. It felt like he worked out too, and I hadn't noticed that when he took me to the florist last week. It made my heart beat oddly just thinking of what he'd look like when he took his shirt off and tossed it in the hamper to climb in his shower.

He led me to a table that seemed very private. There were several others around it, but they were all empty as if he purposefully did that so we'd have less of an audience. We sat, and he pushed in my chair and nodded at the waiter, who dashed off.

I couldn't even articulate how extra this was. I had never in my life been treated this way, and any smidgen of frustration I'd had over being "transformed", as he called it, melted away as he sat across from me and leaned on the table. His eyes met mine, and I felt like he could see through me. Suddenly, the dress felt very immodest. My pulse quickened, and I imagined him undressing me with his eyes. This was a very unbusinesslike business meeting.

"So, Ms. Hart, how are you enjoying the night so far?" James's question seemed to swirl around my head for a few seconds as I tried to collect my thoughts. I really did feel like Cinderella who'd been gifted a fairy godmother to turn me into a princess for this event. Unfortunately for James, the minute this gown came off, I'd turn back into a rag-wearing party planner. It made me feel a bit sad.

"Why are you doing this?" I asked, ignoring his question. I had to know his real motive for bringing me out here. If this was just business, then I was letting my heart and my mind get so carried away, they might not come back to Earth this century.

"I'm treating you the way a woman deserves to be treated, Ms. Hart. Why did you think I asked you here?" His head tilted at an angle, and he blinked slowly. He was testing me. I could see it in his eyes and I didn't know how to respond.

If I told him this was a date, I'd look like a fool when he corrected me. If I told him it was business, I might bruise his ego or worse, turn him away from me. I felt stuck. I didn't like this feeling, especially when my cheeks started to get hot and I thought I would pass out.

Moments passed and no one said anything, and then the waiter brought two glasses of wine and a bottle already chilled. I downed the glass immediately and then took James's glass and downed it too, and he chuckled.

"Relax, Ms. Hart. Let's just talk about something else for the moment." He snapped his napkin and sat back as he draped it over his knee, and I sucked in a breath to calm myself.

He asked me some personal questions and some business questions. I reciprocated and found out he always wanted children but Barbra never wanted to lose her figure. Then I overshared—probably the alcohol—and as we ate, I told him how Mike would micromanage my outfits so I felt a little challenged by Genevieve's stylings.

James graciously apologized and promised to never let that happen again, and we finally fell into a very normal conversation. He loved classical music. I loved to read. He loved sports and I loved crafting. He was an extrovert. I was a seriously hermit-like introvert, but I didn't mind his presence one bit.

When we finished eating, a natural lull in the conversation happened. I almost asked to excuse myself for the restroom, but thanks to the wine and how amazing the company was, I didn't want to leave. My head spun a little, and I figured I'd make a fool of myself by wobbling on these heels Genevieve insisted that I wear with this gown. She wasn't wrong. They were perfect.

"So, Ms. Hart." James steepled his fingers and took on a serious expression. "I want to do more than just take you to dinner. This wasn't the reason I brought you here, but after hearing you talk so passionately about your future, I know it's the right thing. I want to invest in your company."

My throat felt like I got a hunk of that delicious lasagna stuck in it for a second, and I used a gulp of wine to chase it down.

"You what?" I sucked in a breath and set the glass down carefully so it wouldn't spill. I didn't believe what I was hearing.

"I said I want to invest. I want to be a silent partner, though, help you get this new venture off the ground. I won't tell you where to host your offices or what to do, or even what sorts of events to plan or what clients to consult with. I just want you to be successful, and I plan on seeing that through until you are. What do you say?"

I couldn't stop the tears from welling up. They filled my eyes faster than I could blink them back, and I stood up to run away so fast that I almost dumped the whole table on him. James stood too. I heard him moving behind me, barking something at the maître d' as we passed by his station, and I burst into the cold December air with no protection from the wind that bit down on my skin.

James was there instantly. His suitcoat came around my shoulders, and I watched his arm lift into the air. Moments later, the limo was there and I was climbing into the back seat, still crying.

"I'm so sorry, Ivy." My name on his lips only made me cry harder. Why was he being so sweet? Why was he doing this? He couldn't do this. I couldn't let my heart get carried away with another man who promised to make my dreams come true then turned into a monster. This was what happened with Mike, and now it felt like I was falling apart, finally feeling the ache of what that man did to me.

"Shh," James said, pulling me against his body. He wrapped me in a tight hug and kissed my temple. "I'm so sorry."

"Why?" I asked, but he didn't immediately respond. I was overcome with shock and gratitude and yet fear all at once. "Why do this?"

"Isn't it obvious?" he asked, and his eyes searched mine as his hand came up to my face. This time, when his thumb brushed over my skin softly and landed on my bottom lip, I didn't back away.

I felt weak and vulnerable and drunk. I felt like giving him every cell in my being and yet running from him to never let him see that part of my heart that was so fragile, a breath from his lips could break it. But when his lips brushed over mine and my body exploded with scorching desire, I leaned into it.

I kissed him, and I let him kiss me back. His hands pulled me against his mouth, then his body, and I clung to the lapels of his coat. "My God, I've been wanting to do that all night," he said breathlessly when he pulled away, and I was so hungry for some sort of security that I pulled him back.

"Then don't stop," I mumbled as I kissed him again, this time harder.

James responded with equal fervor, his tongue invading my mouth and exploring every inch of it. His hand trailed down my back, grabbing my ass and squeezing it firmly. I moaned into the kiss, arching my back to give him better access. I could feel his erection pressing against my thigh, thick and hard.

When he pulled me onto his lap and the dress hiked up around my waist, I didn't shy away from grinding on his swollen length buried in his pants. His hands were greedy, sliding up and down my back until he found the zipper. In one swoop, he brought it down and the front of the dress loosened. His lips kissed fire down my collarbone to the center of my chest where he used his jaw to nudge the scratchy fabric aside so he could kiss the top of my breast.

My hands ran through his salt-and-pepper hair, and I felt his hands push the length of dress up higher around my waist until he could smooth them around to my ass again. "Mmm," he growled against my nipple as he swirled his tongue around it.

"Shit," I hissed. It felt good to have his hands on me, so damn good. I lost my mind with lust. "God, I want you inside me," I told him breathlessly, and I let my head fall back. My hair was falling loose from the pins Genevieve put in it, but it really came loose when James reached up and grabbed it and held my head at that angle as he sucked my pulse point.

His other hand dipped inside my lacy, black panties, and I gasped. His fingers played with my wet folds. James growled in my ear as he pinched my nipple, sending a jolt of electricity straight to my core.

"Tell me you've been thinking about this all night, too," he demanded, his voice husky with arousal.

"Are you kidding?" I moaned. "I wanted you in that flower shop." I looked down at him and kissed him hard again, and he growled into my mouth. The need in my groin was pulsing, making me climb the walls. I rocked against him, not even caring that the moisture between my legs was probably soaking into his tux pants. I had to take my panties off. I needed to feel him against me.

Clumsily, and a bit drunkenly too, I slid off his lap, and he reached up my dress and tugged my panties down, and before I fell over, I straddled him again, but as I did, he undid his fly and pulled his hard dick out.

"Jesus," I moaned. "You're so big." I wrapped my hand around it and stroked him a couple of times. His breath hitched and he groaned.

"Ivy," he growled, "You're going to make me come before I even get inside you."

I couldn't wait any longer. Guiding his erection to my entrance, I slowly lowered myself onto him. His hands gripped my hips to guide me down as we both moaned together. He was so thick, stretching me in a way that had been a long time since I'd last felt it.

"God, Ivy," he panted as he gripped the headrest behind him. His eyes were squeezed shut and his jaw clenched tightly. "Feels so good."

When I was seated all the way, we both took a moment to catch our breath. Then I started rocking back and forth, riding him slowly at first. James's eyes opened and locked with mine as he began to thrust up into me. Hearing him say my first name suddenly felt so foreign and wrong. I craved the way he'd say, "Ms. Hart," and I knew the moment he did, I'd come apart around him.

I rode him, resting my hands on his shoulders, and then his biceps, and then his chest as my orgasm built. "James," I panted. "Faster."

He obliged and began to pound into me harder and harder. My nails dug into his broad shoulders as his hips ground against mine.

"Oh, God, Ivy," he moaned, "I'm not going to last much longer."

His words were like music to my ears. I felt myself teetering on the edge of orgasm. I was so close, so very close. "Say it," I breathed. "Say my name..." My whimpers felt frantic, but I was so close. It was like my body was waiting for him to push a button that needed pushed.

"You're a goddess, Ivy... So sexy and beautiful."

"No... My name... James." I was so close, so fucking close. I whimpered and opened my eyes, staring at him with eyes wide open as I prayed he'd get my point.

"God, I want to fuck you so hard, Ms. Hart," he said with such confidence it made my entire being detonate.

"Oh, God," I moaned as my orgasm washed over me like a tidal wave. I sank my nails into his shoulders as my pussy clenched around him, and I grunted out his name between clenched teeth. The spasms and convulsions had me draped on him twitching as he pumped in and out of me.

He growled and filled me with his hot seed, his hips thrusting once more before he slowed his thrusts and leaned back against the seat. His chest heaved and mine did too. I was still impaled on him. I couldn't move if I tried. He held me tightly as if not wanting this to end. I didn't want it to end either.

"I'm never going to be able to look you in the eyes at work after this," he joked, panting.

I bit my lip and smiled demurely. "Well, sir," I purred as I sat up and winked at him, "you're not as silent of a partner as you thought."

He chuckled, and I rested my head back on his shoulder. I sniffled, still reeling from that orgasm and the shock of his generous offer. I wasn't sure what to make of any of it. It was all happening so fast. One thing was for sure. I was wasted. I drank way too much wine, and we just had unprotected sex. Neither of those things were good things, but wrapped in his arms, I didn't care. I didn't want to think about what-ifs other than what if this could turn out to be something?

11

JAMES

Ivy lay draped over my chest as the limo rolled up my driveway. I managed to squeeze my hands between our bodies and tuck my limp dick back into my pants. There was a mess, but I'd expected that. I tried to rouse her, but she was well and truly passed out, and part of me wondered how much of what just happened was mutual and how much of it was alcohol.

The driver opened the door as I was getting Ivy situated on the seat next to me. To any other person, it would've looked like I'd given her a drug, but Gus and I had been together for years. He waited for me to climb over her and out of the car, and he stood there while I fixed her dress and picked her up.

"I'd appreciate your discretion, Augustus," I said with a stern expression, and he nodded.

"Of course, Mr. Carver. My lips are sealed." He winked at me. "Unless the police come knocking." His soft chuckle made Ivy smile, but it was a drunken, passed-out grin and her eyes were still shut.

"The door, please," I told him, and he raced ahead of me to open the house door. Genevieve and her crew were long gone. The house was dark. And when I got to Ivy's room, I saw that Marna had left the light on and turned down the bed, though Ivy's room was mostly a scattered mess of belongings haphazardly strewn about. I smiled at it as I laid her on the bed and unzipped the dress.

She moaned as I slid it off her body and draped it over the foot of the bed, and when I stood to admire her curves in the light, she sighed and reached for me with an arm swatting the air. I leaned down to press a kiss to her temple, and she grabbed my tie.

"Fuck me, James," she mewled, but she was too far gone. I'd have happily pinned her to this mattress and fucked her brains out again, but she was a lady, and I was respectful.

"Good night, Ms. Hart," I said as I kissed her cheek. I covered her up, shut off the light, and shut the door as I left.

But I carried a giddy grin on my lips and my chest puffed out a bit farther tonight as I walked toward my bedroom. I took off my soiled pants and threw them in the hamper and noticed Ivy's red suit and bra on my vanity. I smiled as I picked up her bra and looked at it, imagining her nipple in my mouth again. God, that was hot.

But I sighed as I stood under the flow of water and thought about the realities. She was overwhelmed by emotion. That asshole Mike did a number on her confidence and her heart. I could tell she wasn't sure how to take my offer. When she started crying and ran out, the first thought that went through my head was that she thought I was trying to control her future.

I didn't want that at all from her, and I didn't offer to support her business financially just so she'd sleep with me. I wasn't even thinking of that when I made the offer. The way things happened was all on her. She led that moment, and though she was drunk, I did allow it to happen.

Still, as the water washed over my body and I shampooed and rinsed, I thought about how drunk she really was. She wasn't really in any state emotionally to make a choice to start a new relationship. The sex was because of the alcohol and nothing more, and there was a high likelihood that she'd regret it in the morning.

But it was true what I'd said to her. I really would never be able to look at her the same way again, not after that. I really liked the way she made me feel, but it was risky to just hop into bed with someone. It'd only turn into what Barbra and I had, and I'd end up ruining it by being focused on my job instead of her. I doubted Ivy would be the sort of woman to be very forgiving toward a man like that, and it was very hard to teach an old dog new tricks.

I just wanted to see her take off and prove to her old partner that she could do everything she put her mind to without a man bossing her around. She deserved that much. I only hoped the wounds she had from his poor treatment didn't stick around.

I made the decision again to make sure to tell every friend I had how amazing Ivy was and how much she could do for them. And I made that decision because I wanted her to succeed. And in honesty, it was just a good business practice. I'd tell my lawyers to draw up the papers and I'd invest with her, and then all of my word-of-mouth marketing would benefit any return on investment I made.

And I'd get to watch her soar too. Win-win.

12

IVY

My head throbbed so hard, it woke me up. It was cold. I pulled the comforter up over my body higher and snuggled down under it and felt weight across my feet. For a second, I felt a little lost, like I didn't know where I was. My body was so achy and I felt weak, and for some reason, I was naked under the covers.

I blinked my eyes a few times and rubbed them with my fingertips until they adjusted to the light and the room came into focus. I was at James's house, which wasn't a shock, but for some reason, I'd forgotten that I was staying here now and not the hotel. I looked at the nightstand, but my phone wasn't there. Neither was my bra where I normally left it.

Confusion had me sitting up in bed and feeling the moisture between my legs. Then I saw the expensive red dress draped over the foot of the bed and everything started to come back to me—the dress, dinner, the wine... Sex in the back seat of James's limo.

A smile played at my lips as I remembered flashes of the night. It wasn't a clear picture. It came in fuzzy and broken, but the ghost sensation of his stubble scraping across my chest while he sucked on my nipples made me shudder. I'd had sex with Mr. Carver and I enjoyed it.

Then a horrifying reality hit me and I felt dread wash over my body. It wasn't just sex. It was unprotected sex, which was why I was dripping between my legs and still tender. My God, what did I do?

I threw the blankets back and rubbed my face as I heaved out a hard sigh. I'd made some dumb choices in my day, but never one this stupid. Getting pregnant wasn't exactly on my to-do list, but if I was right, there was every chance I was in my fertile days and that thought brought me a bit of panic. I scrambled around the room butt naked looking for my purse and phone. I hadn't taken it with me. There was no point. I was with him, and he paid for everything.

I found my purse under my coat in the armchair in the corner of the room. My phone was on ten percent when I pulled it out of the blankets and opened my health tracker app that helped me log things like my water intake, sleep quality, and most importantly right now, my menstrual cycle. I flicked to it and pressed on the icon, and it only made the dread worse. I was definitely in my fertile time.

"Dammit," I grumbled and I closed my eyes tight. If I got to a pharmacy in the next eight hours, I could potentially get the morning after pill and this would be a non-issue, but I didn't want to freak out and let myself get panicked and carried away.

I plugged my phone in and left it on the nightstand and slunk off to the bathroom to shower. I tried to convince myself that the likelihood of getting pregnant after one night was slim, but my logical mind knew it wasn't impossible. Still, I had a lot riding on my time here with Mr. Carver planning and helping to host his parties. If I sat and obsessed about this too much, I wouldn't be able to manage my workload because I'd be emotionally stressed and worthless to anyone for anything.

The hot water felt amazing washing over my body. I scrubbed myself clean, washed my hair, and rinsed off. Then I let the water just run down over my body and enjoyed the steam fogging the air around me. I touched myself lightly and felt how tender I still was from sex. James must've been big to make me feel this way. I was by no means a virgin, but I felt tender, just like I had the night I lost my virginity.

I wished I hadn't drunk so much. Most of the night escaped me, though I remembered feeling very emotional about something. Though I fully believed the reason I'd had sex with him and not used self-control was due to the alcohol. Had I not drunk so much, I would probably remember things, but maybe the night wouldn't have gone the direction it had.

I swore I heard someone knock on the door, but I stayed under the flow of water. It was probably just Marna asking whether I was going to take breakfast in my room or in the kitchen. It wasn't out of the ordinary for her to do that. But I was enjoying the shower and I didn't want to get out. I wanted to stay here where it was warm and think of James's hands on my body. Every little flash of memory that popped into my mind when I closed my eyes turned me on.

When I got out and dried off, I had to push away a few more thoughts that worried me. If I got pregnant now, it would really throw a wrench in my rebranding. Not only would I feel miserable and be in pain, so my workload would be reduced, but it would mean I had to take weeks off. How would I provide for myself then?

I twisted my hair up in a towel and peeked into my bedroom to make sure Marna wasn't setting up breakfast before I walked in. When I headed toward the bed to see if my phone was charging, I noticed my red suit folded and stacked on the mattress where I'd been lying and a note on my pillow with my name scrawled in messy cursive.

I glanced at the door and then turned back to the bed and realized someone had been in here while I was in the shower, and it didn't appear to be Marna. She wasn't in the habit of leaving notes. Besides, I hadn't even thought of it until just now, but this suit was in James's bedroom, left sitting on the vanity in his bathroom when I put on the gown before he picked me up. My God, he just came into my room while I was in the shower.

I tiptoed over to the door and locked it and then walked back to the bed and sat down. I was freezing, my nipples hard enough to cut glass, but despite the shivering, I picked up the note and unfolded it, and my eyes scanned the slightly neater handwritten text.

Ms. Hart,

I brought your suit back, which was left in my room. I hope you don't mind the intrusion.

I also want to discuss with you the business proposition we spoke about last night. Would you be so kind as to allow my driver to bring you to my office this morning when you are dressed and ready? We could hash out some details of my investment into your firm and what the future might look like.

Yours,

James.

My mind got hung up on the words "investment into your firm" and I stared at them in disbelief. I had zero memory of anyone offering to invest in my firm, let alone James Carver. I was so drunk, this part had been blocked from my memory entirely, but as tears welled up in my eyes at the idea that he'd want to invest with me, I realized that must've been what I was so emotional about.

James wanted to invest in something that was nothing. Mike had kept my name, "Ever After Events", and it pissed me off. But it was pointless to keep a name like that, anyway. I wasn't just planning weddings now. James's idea to help me expand and rebrand meant I'd be planning other parties and events. The former name didn't stick.

And while I was a one-man crew right now, eventually, I'd have a name and an office. I'd hire people to work for me, other planners to do things when I got too busy. That was the dream, but it seemed so far into the future, why would James want to support that? There was nothing. I was literally homeless, living in his house until my jobs for him were done, and then what? I had no place to go, no money to fall back on, no office space. He was an idiot to invest in something that was nothing yet.

It made me feel nervous. Mike had believed in me so much that he took it upon himself to help me get Ever After Events up and running. He poured his own money into the firm and marketed the hell out of my few weddings I had planned. Then he built my portfolio, hired professional photographers. We formed our S-corp and the business took off, but since it was mostly in his name—I was just the talent—now that I left him, he kept it all. I had to start from scratch, including my client lists.

I set the letter down and felt conflicted. The last thing I wanted was for another man to step in and build up a huge business with me, then break my heart and nudge me out. True, I didn't have to give in to Mike. I could've fought him. But I didn't have the money or the means. He'd made sure of that. And right now, I didn't have any way to pass up Mr. Carver's offer to stay here and work for him, so I sort of felt like I was setting myself up for the same scenario.

I had to tell him no. This wasn't going to work. I had to fight to do this on my own. Then when I finally made it someplace, I would know I'd done it on my own hard work and merit, and no one could take it from me.

I dressed in my fanciest suit, which paled in comparison to anything in James's closet. I knew how out of place I'd feel, but he had invited me to discuss this and I had to show up to give him my answer. There was no sense in being embarrassed by who I was or how I dressed, not if I planned to reject his offer and do this on my own, anyway. I had to embrace everything that Ms. Ivy Hart was and embody it to my fullest.

When I walked into the offices of Carver Industries with its towering ceilings and expensive artwork, I felt a lump forming in my stomach. A polite receptionist pointed the way to the elevators and indicated that Mr. Carver was on the sixth floor.

The elevator carried me higher, and I expected to walk onto another floor with another receptionist, but instead I stepped off the elevator into what appeared more like a penthouse. There were windows on all sides, the elevator near the center of the room. The side of the room facing the elevator had a few tables and chairs, a large lounging area with leather sofas, a television, a coffee table, and what appeared to be a bar, with a mirrored and lit backdrop and bottles of expensive whiskey displayed on glass shelves.

"Mr. Carver?" I said as I stepped out and looked around. I turned the corner, and as I walked I saw more of the space that took up the entire sixth floor. A large mahogany desk sat all the way in the far corner of the room with a view of the bay out the windows that took my breath away. In the other corner were a small kitchenette and another table. And right behind the elevators was a huge conference table, at which James sat with another man.

Both of them stood and nodded at me as I came into view. James had a soft smile on his face, but the other man looked stern and very businesslike.

"Hello," I said softly.

"Welcome, Ms. Hart. Come, sit down." James gestured at the chair next to his, and I glanced at the other man nervously. I wasn't aware that anyone else would be here, but it made sense. I was just in awe of this whole experience. Even the floor cost more than my entire net worth.

"Ms. Hart, this is Mr. Bronwyn Sutter, my attorney. He's here to help us iron out the entire agreement and make sure you're covered." James sat down as I lowered myself nervously into the chair. He already had his lawyer drawing up a contract, and that made the knot in my gut tighten.

"Mr. Carver, I must say I'm surprised." I felt my cheeks heating up, and I winced at how cowardly I sounded.

"Surprised by this invitation? Or my office?" He chuckled, and the lawyer cracked a smile as he spun his legal notepad around and slid it across the table toward me. I glanced down at it, but his writing was messy. I could barely make out a sum of two million dollars, and that made my eyes want to pop out.

"Uh, everything," I breathed, trying to focus on the words to read them. Once again, my brain hurt. "What's this?" I asked, looking up at James with a bit of terror coursing through my body.

"We're making a list of our terms. I want you to add anything there you feel like you might want." He used a finger to tap on the notepad and then he smiled at me. "I've already had him list a few things, as you can see."

"I can't read this," I told him, feeling overwhelmed.

"Ms. Hart, I apologize. My handwriting is quite messy at times." The lawyer took his pad back and started reading. "Mr. Carver has offered the sum of two million for dispersal upon acceptance of his investment. He will provide business acumen, counseling, marketing coordination, and legal services as you get started for a period of two years. He asks nothing in return and gives you full decision-making power."

My eyes hurt. I rubbed them and blinked a few times and turned to James, feeling like I was going to cry. He was smiling so brightly, I felt bad even thinking about telling him no. This wasn't a five-thousand-dollar kick start. This was millions of dollars at my disposal from a man I'd only just met. This felt like a trap.

"I know what you're thinking, Ms. Hart, but I want to assure you that this isn't a trick. You came along at a time in my life when I thought I was going to fall apart, and you have already taught me a few things that have changed my life for the good." James splayed his palms on the table in front of him. "I want to help you the same way."

"I don't know what to say." Everything in me was screaming *run away*, but I stayed seated. Two million dollars was a lot of money to walk away from.

"You don't have to say anything. I am telling you this money and all of my help are yours, with no obligation. You don't even have to pay it back. I believe in your talents and services, and I fully believe you're going to go places. I want you to have the financial security to really explore this rebranding you're doing and let the entrepreneurial part of your heart blossom. Just say yes and tell me what terms or conditions you have."

I forced myself not to cry, though I really wanted to.

I spent the rest of that entire day going over details. We hashed out a loose contract to revisit in a few days. We looked at properties on realty websites both in and out of Green Bay and Lover's Bay, and we had lunch and a few cocktails later that afternoon to celebrate the collaboration. With James's lawyer assuring me that the offer really was as generous as it sounded, I felt confident signing on the dotted line, and at the end of the day, this was business, not personal.

And I almost forgot about the unprotected sex too. Until my head was on my pillow and I was turning in for the night. I decided it was a tomorrow problem as I drifted off to sleep feeling grateful for Mr. Carver and how much he believed in me.

Now if I could get the idea of fucking him again out of my head, we'd be good. Strangely, we were entirely comfortable all day, not one awkward moment. Maybe I just dreamed up the sex… but why did I wake up naked, then?

13

JAMES

The meal on the table in front of me was delicious—I'd have returned it had it been low quality—but I felt hollow. I'd been in Chicago for the past week on an unavoidable business trip. Each year, this tech conference came up, introducing the latest innovations that would hit store shelves in the following year but featuring options for folks to buy for Christmas that current year. This year, I was a spotlight speaker, which meant there was an even greater demand on me to be present.

But I felt alone.

Since the first week of November when Ivy moved into my home and started planning my events for me, we'd taken dinner together almost every evening. There were a few times when I had other obligations and once when she visited her family near Thanksgiving, but the routine of having our evening meal together had been set.

Tonight, hundreds of miles from home, I missed the banter and exchange of speaking with her over our meal. She had a way of helping me end my day on a high note, and after being exhausted by speaking and sharing all day and walking around looking at other companies' progress in the industry, I felt like the grumpy version of myself that Barbra left.

I stabbed the steak with my fork and brought it to my mouth and let the savory meat melt on my tongue as I thought about Ivy Hart straddling my hips and me devouring her. She'd been so drunk that night, I knew it was borderline inappropriate. And in fact, she acted so natural around me following that night—never once bringing it up—that I feared it had even escaped her memory. I didn't have the guts to fully bring it up in case she felt like I'd crossed a line. It was the farthest thing from my mind.

But I remembered.

God, did I remember—every little detail. I doubted she'd have thrown herself at me like that if she were sober, though. I'd made it very clear to her how much of a failure I thought I was in my marriage. I had spelled it out in detail how I ignored Barbra and left her neglected at home while I worked my fingers to the bone. Any woman with a head on her shoulders would run for the hills, which only told me that if Ms. Hart were actually interested in me, it was for my body. It clearly wasn't for my money. She was shellshocked and hesitant when it came to my investing in her firm. I thought I was going to have to twist her arm to accept my money.

But bodies break down, and I felt like an old man. The greys at my temple told anyone my age. There was no logical reason a twenty-something would want to date a man my age, even if they did get turned on while drunk and throw themselves at me. Ms. Hart deserved a man who would cherish her, one without hangups and flaws. I had to get it out of my head that she was interested in me for a relationship and realize that what happened only happened due to the wine she'd consumed and had nothing to do with me as a person.

But my dinner time was still lonely. I'd managed to keep myself busy the entire week so I didn't miss the interaction as much. I knew if I let myself get so used to the routine that I was missing her after a few days, when she left my home in February after the Valentine's Day event, the real loneliness and isolation would settle in. I had to break the habit soon, settle in to my life of mourning a lost marriage.

I just didn't want to start that yet.

So I picked up my phone and called her. Any other trip, I'd have called Barbra to see how she was doing. The call would be flat and dry. She'd list off the shows she watched on TV or the decorations she put up around the house. I'd tell her how my meetings were boring and I wished I were home. We'd fall silent and the call would end. But the instant the line connected, I knew this call with Ivy would be different.

"James," she said, sounding breathless. "Sorry, I'm just getting a workout in. What can I do for you?" She was panting, and I pictured her glistening with sweat wearing nothing but a sports bra and spandex, just like that morning in my kitchen.

"I apologize, Ms. Hart. I was just calling to check on how things are going…" *And to hear your voice*, I should've added, but I didn't. As much as I wanted to, I had to restrain myself from pursuing her. She deserved a young man with his whole life ahead of him, not someone like me.

"Things are great. The work party went well. Sam's a sweet guy. He helped me get everything finished up. And things are on track for your party here, too. I have the whole house decorated, and I even had them put up lights outside—don't worry. Very classy. Nothing tacky." She snickered, and the tinkling of her laughter made me smile.

"You are so beautiful when you smile," I said aloud, and I instantly wished I hadn't. Picturing her with a smile on her lips was a bad idea because it made me talk without thinking, but she really was beautiful.

"James," she said in a tone that suggested she was embarrassed or discouraging my comment. Or maybe she just had a hard time accepting compliments. Some people were like that.

I looked forward to seeing many more smiles on her face too—when she finally picked her name for her company, when it became a reality, settling in to a new office space, buying her first company car. There were so many firsts ahead along with the smiles to match them, and I had assured myself a front row seat by investing. I wasn't sure whether that was going to be good for my heart or not, but it was a fact now.

"It's true," I said softly. And to save myself, I added, "And you do fantastic work."

There was a pause on the line as I heard her catching her breath, and then she spoke. "I never got a chance to fully thank you for your offer to invest. I think I was so overwhelmed by emotion, I lost myself for a while. It's been strange not having you here, but I should have offered my gratitude a long time ago."

I knew without a doubt that she had lost herself, and I had too. We'd done it together that night in my limo, and watching her face as she came undone around me was exquisite, the most beautiful I'd ever seen her.

"I think you showed me your gratitude already... though that wasn't necessary." My heavy insinuation that the sex was her gratitude toward me was wrong. I knew it was. I shouldn't have said it. I didn't want her to think I had offered to invest just to get her in bed with me. Hell, I didn't even know if she remembered a thing about it.

"I, uh..." I thought she was going to end the call and run, but she continued and it surprised me in a nice way. "I had a really great time that night."

I smiled, wishing I could see the expression on her face. "I think it was one of the top ten greatest nights of my life." That was a phrase I wasn't ashamed to say because it was true.

"Uh, I should... I need to finish my workout." She sounded flustered, and I pictured that blush spreading across her cheeks.

"Goodnight, Ms. Hart. Sleep well." I heard her mumble a quick goodbye, and I ended the call.

Dammit, my heart was getting carried away and I knew it shouldn't. She was just so perfect, and I wanted to make all of her dreams come true. Which was why I had to get control of myself because I knew dating a man who was already halfway to the grave wasn't on her list of top ten greatest things of her life.

Ivy Hart was incredible, and incredibly out of my league.

14

IVY

The Christmas lights were so pretty, but nothing compared to the centerpieces I had selected for James's Christmas Eve celebration only nine days away now. I loved the way crystalized sugar made the pinecones appear as if snow clung to the woody scales. And the frosted-glass candle holders would finish the look of elegance. I knew James's guests would be impressed.

I also knew how much pressure I was under to make sure everything was perfect, and the pressure just kept getting worse as days passed. Not only did I have to pull off these final few events and plan the event of a lifetime on Valentine's Day, but I had to come up with a company name, a business plan, and juggle the stress of apartment hunting. And on top of all of that, I was sort of freaking out.

My period was late—two days, to be exact. I took two pregnancy tests already, but neither of them were positive, so I should've just been able to relax and put it behind me, but my period was never late. Even when I was horribly stressed, I was regular like clockwork. It wasn't a good sign for me, and I couldn't shake the feeling that my life was about to change.

"The lights look beautiful," I heard, and I knew the rumble of James's baritone voice before I even turned to look at him. I stood in my messy workspace cluttered with all the decorations from the past few parties on one side and things I was putting together for his future events on the other. I was a bit embarrassed at how disorganized it looked, but I had a system. I knew where everything I needed was.

"Thank you," I said, turning slowly to face him. "I've been working nonstop." I bit my lip, hoping he approved of everything, not just the lights. I knew it was very different from what his former wife did. His staff didn't let me forget it. She used traditional things like snowmen and gingerbread men, and every color in the rainbow. I chose plain white lights, plaids and creams, and my favorite part was the abundance of reindeer, stashed here and there, indoors and out. It was classy, like James.

"I can tell," he said, looking around. "You've been a busy little elf." He grinned and walked over to me and looked down at my first finished centerpiece and smiled at it. "This is nice too."

"I'll have twelve tables, each with a centerpiece like this. I think they'll look nice," I told him, and I picked up a length of red ribbon I intended to turn into a bow to fashion around the candle, but it slipped from my hand and fell to the floor. I almost bent to retrieve it, but James got to it first. I remembered that day in the florist shop where something similar had happened and thought better of it. I didn't need a concussion to add to my stress.

But the moment did remind me of that almost kiss we shared. I wished I remembered more from that night in his limo the way I had let that moment at the florist imprint on my mind. My body flushed as I remembered the few things that were stored in my memory, namely how his lips and stubble felt on my chest.

"Looks like you dropped this," he said as he handed me the ribbon. I took it from his hand and smiled shyly.

I'd been caught red-handed daydreaming about him, and while I should've been obsessing about whether or not I was pregnant, I found myself being drawn to him again. Only this time, I was sober.

"You know, we never did talk about..." I couldn't finish. How would I ever bring up the thought that I could be pregnant? I knew nothing for certain, but there was a chance. And it rattled me. James should know too.

"What do you feel like you should say to me?" he asked, but it wasn't dismissive. I could tell he actually wanted to know what I was thinking, and suddenly, the only thing I was thinking of was kissing him again. I shouldn't have been thinking that at all, ever, because he was my boss, a client, an investor, almost twice my age, and just a bad idea all around. But I enjoyed his presence.

James was a sweet, caring man. He was thoughtful and generous. We got along and had things in common. And no one had ever made me feel so supported or encouraged.

"I... Uh, I don't know." The truth slipped out of my mouth and I shrugged. We should talk about the fact that we had sex, but we moved on like nothing happened. Maybe because he thought I didn't remember. Or maybe because he felt like it was a mistake or he was ashamed of it?

"I think we both know we enjoyed it..." He stepped closer, and I smelled his cologne. It was intoxicating.

"Well, yes, but..." I felt flustered with him so close to me.

"And what's done is done. No changing that." His hand rested on the table in front of us and moved closer to mine, and I felt the air charge with chemistry.

"James," I breathed, and I felt myself getting worked up. An ache started low in my groin. I knew he hadn't come in here to flirt with me. He came to check on my work, but I wanted him. I wanted to feel what he made me feel that night in his limo—the feelings I couldn't quite remember. The ones that visited me in my dreams.

"Ms. Hart," he said, as if waiting for me to say or do something. My breathing was thready and shallow. My heart was pounding.

"I feel…" I fanned myself, but I didn't back away when his hand rose up and cupped my cheek.

"Flustered?" he asked, and I bit my lip and hid a smirk.

His fingers curled around the back of my neck and he pulled me a few inches closer. "Is this alright?" he asked, and I nodded.

"It's okay," I told him.

"Why me?" he whispered, and his eyes searched my face. I couldn't answer him. There was no reason I should be so attracted to him, but I was.

"Why not?" I asked, bobbing one shoulder, and he closed the gap and pressed his lips against mine.

The kiss was scorching, every bit as delicious as I thought it would be. In a sober state, I was able to enjoy every brush of his lips across mine, the way he held me in place with his hand, and the way his tongue slipped across mine. And when he pulled back, leaving me breathless, I felt drunk on endorphins.

"I'm going to need you to do that thing again so I can remember it this time." My eyes were hooded with lust, and he grinned as he leaned in and whispered in my ear.

"Do what thing again?" he whispered, and it made goosebumps rise on my arms.

"Fuck me," I whispered back, and the vixen inside me was unleashed.

He chuckled and bent his head low and kissed me again. This time, it was more urgent, hungrier, and I felt my body responding to him in a way I never thought possible. His hands roamed my curves, gripping my hips and lifting me onto the table. He pressed me against the smooth surface, and I wrapped my legs around his waist.

His lips left mine and blazed a trail down my neck, along my collarbone, and to the valley between my breasts. He unbuttoned my shirt, and it pooled around my waist on the table, along with my bra, which he removed. My breasts spilled out, and he cupped one in his warm hands, teasing the nipple with his thumb.

"Is this what you want?" he asked, his voice low and deep in my ear.

"Yes," I gasped, arching my back to him. "More."

He complied, trailing kisses down my stomach, leaving a fiery trail in his wake. His hands were everywhere, skilled and sure, as if he had done this a million times before. But when he looked up at me through his lashes, I knew this was anything but practice for him. His fingers worked the zipper of my slacks and he unbuttoned them, then he stood and undid his own shirt. I sat there leaning back on my hands, watching him.

"You're staring," he said, teasing me with his eyes as he unbuttoned his pants. His chest was bare and it was gorgeous. His muscles were toned, and the trail of hair leading into his waistband tempted me. It made my core ache for what I knew was inside his boxers.

"I like what I see," I purred, and he smirked and stepped forward.

"Well, then, let me show you more." James hooked his fingers into the waistband of my slacks and panties and pulled, and I lifted myself slightly so he could pull them down and off.

I sat on the table in front of him as he pulled his dick out of his fly and stroked it. His eyes scanned up and down my body, but my eyes were on his cock. I was right. He was thick. It was the reason my pussy ached for a full day after fucking him the first time.

"Wow," I mumbled, and before I lost myself entirely, I looked him in the eye. "Condom." I wouldn't make the same mistake twice.

"I came prepared," he said, smirking, and I smiled.

"Then, what are we waiting for?" I asked, spreading my legs wider for him.

"Patience," he purred.

James stepped forward and rested his hands on my thighs as he leaned down to kiss me again. I reached for his dick and gripped him, stroking lightly as I imagined how this thick tool would feel inside me. I clenched around nothing, already whimpering for penetration.

But James had other plans. He kissed my neck, then down my chest, then lower still to my aching core. His tongue lapped at the sensitive bud between my legs, sending a jolt of electricity through me. I bucked against him, moaning his name as his tongue flicked over my clit.

"Oh, God," I panted, gripping the table for support as he worked his magic on me. "Oh, God, yes," I moaned, and he chuckled against my wet folds.

"You like that?" he asked, and I whimpered in response.

"Yes," I gasped out. "More."

He obliged me, sucking on my clit while his fingers delved inside me, stretching me out for him. My body shuddered, and the orgasm built inside me.

"Shit," I swore. "Fuck, I'm so close."

"That's what I like to hear," he mumbled against my skin, and I felt him chuckle as he lapped at me. My eyes rolled back in my head, and I was a mass of goo in his hands.

"James," I moaned, "I'm gonna—"

He lightly bit down on my swollen nub, and I came apart in his mouth, grunting his name as my pussy clenched around his magical fingers. I convulsed and twitched, and he mercilessly finger fucked me until I was jolting and whimpering. When my orgasm subsided, he stood and nestled between my thighs.

"Your turn," he whispered, and I reached out to grip his thick length.

"Condom," I reminded him, panting.

"I got it," he said, and he reached into his back pocket and pulled out a condom. He sheathed himself, and then he was back between my legs, ready to fuck me into another orgasm.

"Are you ready for this?" he asked, and I nodded.

"Yes," I breathed. "Oh, God, James," I moaned as he filled me up, stretching me in ways that made my toes curl. He took his time, easing himself into me, then he started to move, slowly at first, then he picked up speed until the room was filled with only our moans.

"Fuck," I swore, and he chuckled again.

"You like that?" he asked, and I bit my lip.

"Don't stop," I moaned, and he didn't.

He pounded into me, ramming his cock so deep inside me I thought I would split in half. His hands gripped my thighs, and he held on as if his life depended on it.

"Touch me. Touch my clit. Do it," I pleaded, and he moved his hand until he was gripping my hip and his thumb was rubbing my clit.

"Like this?" he asked, and I moaned in response.

"Yes," I gasped. "Don't stop."

The combination of his dick inside me and his thumb on my clit had me coming apart again. This time, it was so much more intense than before. My pussy clenched around him, and I screamed his name as he grunted and came inside the condom.

We were both panting for air when it was over, and he collapsed against my chest, and I wrapped my arms around him. For a moment, it didn't feel bad or wrong or even awkward. It felt like two people who were crazy hot for each other who just had incredible sex.

But his phone rang, breaking the trance, and when he pulled out and backed away, I sat there naked on his table in front of him feeling embarrassed and ashamed. He pulled his phone out of his pocket, and still winded, he held up a finger to me and answered it.

"James Carver..."

I didn't hear what the person on the other end was saying, but I watched his face contort into a scowl.

"I'll be there shortly. Don't do anything."

James hung up and turned back to me, stepping up to kiss me fiercely again. "I have to go. My God, you're beautiful..." He kissed me again and said, "I'm not sure what's happening here, Ms. Hart, but I like this. And if you just happen to turn up in my bed tonight, I won't chase you away." Then he kissed me again and walked toward the door.

He stopped and took the full condom off his dick, then he zipped up and left the room, leaving me breathless and speechless.

Why the hell couldn't I control myself around him? And what was really happening? Did I even want to know? Was James the new Mike and I just didn't know it yet?

15

JAMES

When the elevator dinged and the doors slid open, I looked up from my desk to see Mr. Sutter walking in. He carried his briefcase and a cup of coffee, and he had a determined expression on his face.

"Bronwyn, come on in." I stood and pushed aside the contract I was reviewing and reached across my desk to shake his hand as he sat down. The space felt hollow and cold today, one week until Christmas, but the atmosphere changed when he smiled and clicked open his briefcase.

"James, I have good news for you." He reached into his case and extracted a manilla file folder and slid it across my desk. His slight nod as I picked it up and opened it was encouraging.

Any "good news" from my lawyer was welcome. After the past month of stressing out over Barbra's annulment request and what it would mean for my future, I was ready to put it behind me and get on with my life. The shift in my thinking that had been agonizingly slow in coming happened when Ivy freed me from my ridiculous archaic mindset. Now I was ready to finish the process by finalizing everything.

I sat slowly as I looked over the conditions of the annulment. Barbra was asking for a hefty alimony check every month, but thankfully, she didn't try to stake any claim to my company. She'd have lost the battle, but it would've drawn things out for months. If ten thousand a month got her away from me so I could start over, so be it.

"So it's done? All I have to do is sign this?" I looked up from the paperwork, and Bronwyn nodded.

"That's it. The judge will review everything and get back with us with his judgement. It'll take a month or so, but hopefully, we'll be finished with all that nonsense by the end of January." He narrowed his eyes at me and asked, "Are you sure you're okay? I'm not a typical family law guy, but you seem to be breezing through this quite easily."

My chest constricted at his question. Bronwyn wasn't just my lawyer. He was also a family friend. He'd been at my wedding. He was there when Barbra miscarried that one time, after which she got her tubes tied. And he'd been with me every step of the way building this company. Of course he would know me well enough to know this should've been destroying me, if not for my secret reason. Ms. Ivy Hart.

I thought about it for a second, but there really was no other way to explain why I was handling this so well. He was right. I should've been falling apart, wrestling with my part in this and blaming myself. But I'd done that for the past nine months. I didn't want to do that anymore. She wanted her freedom, so I was cutting her loose.

"I think the past nine months have been long enough for me to say I don't need to break down about this anymore." I smiled and set the folder on my desk, then took out a pen, signed the paper, and handed the file back to him. "Done, and done." I nodded as he took it and put it back into his briefcase.

"There's more..." He pulled another folder out of his briefcase, this one yellow. I raised my eyebrows as he tossed it onto my desk then closed his case and set it on the ground. "It's the draft for our contract with Ms. Hart and her business, which by the way, I strongly recommend not signing until you've seen her business plan. We have to be sure what we're getting into with—"

"It's fine," I said dismissively as I opened the folder and let my eyes pore over the words on the page. This contract interested me far more than the annulment paperwork, as this was my future. I wasn't looking back on something that was crumbling apart. I was looking forward to my future, and it encouraged me.

"James, I'm just trying to do my due diligence with this. Pouring this much money into a company that has no name, no business plan, no structure... It's not a great idea." Bronwyn tapped his fingers on the arm of the chair on which he sat, and I was reminded that as my good friend, he was just doing his job.

I lifted my eyes from the file and sighed. "I understand what you're saying, but you don't have all the details. Ms. Hart ran a very successful firm and only recently parted ways with it to take on this new venture." The fine details weren't mine to share with my lawyer. I wasn't about to tell him how her boyfriend treated her or why she felt the need to leave.

And given my knowledge of growing a startup from the ground up, and the resources I had at my disposal, I was personally willing to guarantee that Ivy wouldn't fail. I just had a few legal questions to run past him. I wasn't really interested in his protective personal opinion.

"James, be smart. You have a lot of money. I could use it as insulation in the walls of my home, but do you really want to throw it at this woman?" He narrowed his eyes at me skeptically and pursed his lips. "You're sleeping with her... and Barbra only just left."

To those in my inner circle who saw any of this, they'd assume the same thing and they'd be right. And for the first time in my life, I didn't care about anyone's opinion at all. I wanted to support Ivy and help her. I knew there was a very low probability that anything would ever work out, and it didn't change my mind at all. Even if she went her way and nothing ever amounted to anything except the amazing sex we'd had, I still wanted to support her.

"Barbra fucked her yoga instructor, Bron. I think I deserve to have a little fun." I winced at how that sounded, as if I were using Ivy as my blow-up doll. Which couldn't have been further from the truth. I sighed hard and rubbed my face. "She left. It's over. I don't think there is some waiting period I'm supposed to uphold, is there? She never stopped sleeping with him, and I'm pretty sure she moved in with him. I think I can move on."

He massaged the bridge of his nose and said, "Just be careful."

"Is there some ethical thing I should know about? I'm giving her two million dollars without any strings attached except for that two percent of her profits she forced me to write in. If we're interacting on a social level... Let's say you're right and we're screwing. Does that mean I can't invest?"

He lowered his hand and sighed and shook his head. "No. It doesn't preclude you from being an investor, but it's tricky ethically. You have to make sure this is a true intimate thing between you or things could get messy... Lawsuits over harassment and... James, she could take your whole company if it goes pear-shaped."

In my gut, I knew Bronwyn was right, but in my heart, I wanted to believe Ivy wasn't that person. She and I sparked, nothing more. I sincerely wanted to see her succeed, so if it ended with her taking advantage of me just so she could get a leg up, I'd gladly give her anything she asked for. I wasn't doing this to be manipulative. I was doing this to help her. It was what I actually wanted.

I decided that if I put good into the world, it would come back to me. And that was the position I was holding to.

Still, I knew it was tricky, just like my lawyer said. Even if Ivy wasn't the harlot Bronwyn suggested she could be, I still had to be careful. My heart was getting involved. I was caring about her far more than a business partner should, and she could get hurt too. That was the last thing I wanted for her, more heartbreak. Maybe I was going a bit too far. Maybe I should back off.

16

IVY

I walked around the small store front that overlooked the bay, and I loved it. The spacious offices were way more than enough room for me to make my plans, though the storage in back would be tight, but it had designated parking in the lot out front and the view of Lover's Bay out the window was to die for.

"It's hideous," Kevin grumbled. "You'll have thirty grand in repairs and upgrades to even make this place usable." He turned up his nose to this one too. Every single commercial property up for rent that we'd visited today either completely turned me off or made Kevin cringe. I was starting to get upset with him over every comment he made.

I winced and avoided eye contact with Ms. Pratt, the realtor who'd been showing us around for the day. She was a pleasant woman, but even I could tell that Kevin was pushing her patience to its limits. She had several more properties for us to check out, though I'd have been satisfied with a few I'd already seen. It almost made me wish I hadn't brought Kevin along.

"I don't know. It's got charm," I said, already picturing the new flooring and window covers. The storefront could host portfolios of all my previous events and examples of my decorations. Besides, it was far enough away from Mike that I didn't have to worry about overlap and competition.

"Green Bay is far better. You've got to know that." Kevin folded his arms over his chest, and I noticed the relator scowl before she turned away.

"What the hell is wrong with you?" I hissed under my breath, and he rolled his eyes.

"What's wrong with me is that you're purposefully self-sabotaging." The way he spoke to me sounded a whole lot like the way Mike used to speak to me, and I didn't like it at all.

"I like this place," I said in a whisper, and he shook his head.

"It's not move-in ready. It's got no store space, and no storage. And it's not central. Look out that window—"

"It's called a view," I spat and huffed. Then I squared my shoulders and turned to Ms. Pratt. "I think we can move on to the next one."

She nodded at me, avoiding even looking at Kevin, and said, "Come this way…" She led us back out to her cute little BMW convertible, and we climbed in. The heat was cranked up, but I was so frigid. Between Kevin's cold treatment and the chill in the air five days until Christmas, I wondered if I'd ever warm up again.

"So, where is the next one?" I asked, purposefully ignoring the way Kevin sat in the back seat sighing loudly. He was pissed, but he wasn't in charge. I bet he hated that too, that he had no say. Mike never gave him any say, but up until now, I'd let him push me around. I let both of them do that. But this money given to me by James had to go a long way. Two million sounded like a lot, but with rent priced at three to four thousand a month, I needed to ensure my space was perfect and able to start making me a profit immediately.

"Oh, it's on the south side closest to Door County. You're going to love this one." She smiled at me and pulled her car into traffic, and I heard Kevin snort before he scoffed.

"South side? You're trying to get even farther away from the center of the real business?" I winced at his comment and felt like telling him off right there in front of her. He was being so rude and I'd had enough.

"Well, I'm going to buy a van, anyway. I need one. I can't keep using Mike's." I kept my eyes trained on the road as Ms. Pratt drove and cringed when Kevin started in on me again.

"You know Ever After didn't buy a van until the third year. What are you trying to do, fail on purpose? Ivy, you have no clue how to run a business and—"

"Shut up!" I shouted, and I watched Ms. Pratt bite back a smirk. I gritted my teeth and blinked back tears of anger. Then I turned over my shoulder and glared at him. "Ever After started with five grand and struggled to get off the ground. Event Queen is starting off with millions in the back in capital, and I'm going to start out strong."

He scrunched his nose up and pulled his head back so his neck wrinkled up and then made a gagging face. "That's the name you're going with? Event Queen? Are you insane?"

Tears welled up, and I turned to Ms. Pratt. "Please stop the car," I told her, and she nodded at me. It took a few blocks, but she found a parking spot and pulled into it and I turned over my shoulder. "You can get out now, Kevin. I don't need your help anymore."

He scoffed loudly, and Ms. Pratt covered her mouth with her hand to hide a smirk again. "You can't do that. Do you have any idea how much an Uber back to Green Bay will cost from here?"

"Apparently, it's the cost of our friendship." I clenched my jaw shut, and he scoffed again, but he climbed out and slammed the door.

Ms. Pratt didn't immediately pull away, and the tears came hot and fast. All I wanted was for someone to believe in me, and it took the kindness of a complete stranger to make me break.

"Are you alright?" she said softly, touching my elbow as I wiped tears from my eyes. She reached into her glove box and pulled out a brown paper napkin.

"Yeah, he's just really awful sometimes." I blew my nose, and she sighed.

"Let me take you home. We can do this again another day. I'll find more properties that will be perfect for you." She smiled softly, and I nodded.

The ride was quiet and she was patient with me. I was humiliated, but I knew I'd go back to her. I did love a few of the properties, and I could see myself setting up shop there, even if Kevin thought Green Bay would be better for me than Lover's Bay. And I knew I could be successful because James's help wasn't just financial. He was going to coach me through the whole process.

Which was the only reason I had enough motivation to get my room cleaned up and finish a bit of last-minute decorating around the Carver Estate. I had to show him how seriously I was taking his investment into my future. I couldn't let Kevin ruin this for me.

17

JAMES

Ivy had been a little distant the past few days, even when I invaded her space to ask questions about the Christmas dinner I was hosting. I didn't pry, and I didn't push her to talk, but I did feel partly to blame. It was Christmas Eve, and instead of being at home with her family where she should have been, she was at my house finishing plans and making sure the event staff were coordinated.

Years past, I'd watched Barbra float around the house and bark orders, and I knew it was possible for Ivy to handle everything on her own, but it was my party, not hers. I should have been the one there doing the last-minute arrangements. She was just the planner and coordinator. I was the host.

And as the host, I wanted to make sure she felt valued for her part in this. Yes, I paid her, but after everything she'd been through and the fact that it was Christmas, I felt compelled to buy her a trinket to show my gratitude.

"This one is beautiful," the petite woman with dark hair standing behind the jewelry counter said. She held a barrette in her hand. The gems on it sparkled and danced under the light, and her smile was as bright as the twinkles.

"It is pretty..." I said, but I wasn't sure it was quite perfect. I had my eye on the barrette that was shaped like a butterfly and dripped with diamonds. It probably cost more than Ivy's entire wardrobe, but it was simple enough that she could pull it off without anyone knowing it wasn't paste. I'd have bought her an entire new wardrobe if she'd let me, but I didn't want her to think she wasn't enough the way she was.

"What about that one?" I asked, pointing at the one I had in mind, and she clicked her tongue and set the other one down on the glass display.

"It's for someone special, then?" she asked as she reached into the case. "You realize this is nearly three carats in princess cut diamonds? They're natural..." Her eyes swept up to my face, and I lifted my eyebrows in annoyance. It wasn't often that my word was questioned, but this woman didn't know me. This impromptu visit hadn't been scheduled.

"I'm not sure..." I told her, questioning my own reason for buying this. Ivy was special, just not in the way this woman insinuated. At least I didn't think. So we had sex a few times, and sure, we hit it off in conversation every time. But even when I questioned her about what was going on between us, neither of us had a clue.

We'd both just gotten out of bad relationships, and more than anything, I just wanted to see her succeed. My heart was invested in making her happy, helping build her company and confidence, and allowing her to be herself without any strings attached.

I plucked the barrette from her hand and turned it back and forth under the lights. I pictured it in Ivy's beautiful warm brown hair and smiled. She would look stunning.

"Sir, this barrette costs forty grand. She'd better be special, or you're a fool." Her chuckle, followed by a snort, told me she really had no clue who I was. I laid it back on her palm and straightened. I took my wallet out and slid my Visa across the display case with one finger.

"I'll take it, and add gift wrapping too, please."

Her eyes grew wide as she looked down at the card and back up to my face. "I'm so sorry, Mr. Carver, I didn't..." She swallowed hard and shook her head. "I'll take care of this right away, sir," she said as she scurried off with my card.

I chuckled at her being so flustered and thought of Ivy when she got flustered. The way her lips would flush dark and her cheeks would brim with crimson. It made me smile like a fool in love, and I realized I was. I was starting to fall in love, or what I thought was love back at one point in time. The rush of excitement to be around her, the giddiness over how she turned me on and made me feel young again.

But I couldn't get carried away or let my heart feel this. This wasn't love. I learned that from Ivy. Love was more than hormones and chemistry. It was commitment, and something deeper, something mysterious I couldn't put my finger on yet. I just knew what I wanted —to keep that smile on her face as much as possible.

"Here we are, sir," the woman said when she returned. She slid my card back to me with a receipt. Then she showed me the options for wrapping paper and gift boxes. There were ribbons and cards and even gift tags to choose from, and I stood there for a good thirty minutes, agonizing over everything when finally, she said, "Well, for as much as you're fussing over this, that woman must be special. If a man did this for me, I'd marry him."

She waltzed away with my final selections, leaving a warmth in my chest I couldn't shake. I didn't think of this as a romantic gesture. I just wanted it to be perfect so that when Ivy opened it, her eyes would fill with tears and she would feel like the strong, capable woman she was. I wanted to see her smile, and I wanted her to feel beautiful and confident every time she clipped it in her hair.

I spent the entire ride home knowing I would give this to her tomorrow, and now my agony was different. What if she hated it? What if she thought I was being manipulative by giving her expensive gifts? She was a simple woman with simple tastes. Perhaps the less expensive emerald barrette would have been better.

Or worse... What if she had the same reaction that woman had? What if Ivy thought this was a declaration of love? What if I was sending a signal I wasn't quite ready to send?

I hated how I always overthought everything. And I hated how every action could be judged individually and interpreted differently by different people. This was just a thank you gift, right? I was just trying to support and encourage a woman who was very down on her luck, nothing more.

So why did my heart feel like I wanted Ivy to react the way that woman said she'd have reacted?

18

IVY

"Yes, and take the stuffing out too." I kept getting asked questions, and as fast as they came at me, I offered answers. I hired a catering staff of twenty. James's "intimate gathering" was nearly forty people. The string quartet was on their ten-minute break while people continued to eat, so I had Christmas music humming softly through a speaker I'd set up.

James sat at the head of the table smiling and sipping his wine while dinner was being served, but my plate of food sat on the counter in the kitchen waiting for me. I purposefully hadn't given myself a seat at the table because I wasn't officially one of James's friends or family. Recently, we'd been so busy, I didn't even know what we were.

When he asked me what was going on between us, my only response was to ask him if it mattered. I had no clue what to tell him. I was falling for him so hard, but I couldn't decipher whether it was actual real emotion or if it was my being on the rebound. Add to that the fact that he was a gazillionaire and super hot, and it was a tangled mess to try to sort out. I sort of wished I'd listened to Kevin when he told me staying here was a bad idea.

"Ms. Hart, the quartet is preparing for their next set. You should go eat." Marna smiled at me softly as she touched my hand. She was used to serving James and his guests, and to her this event was more relaxing than normal. I'd done all the heavy lifting for everyone, and more than one of James's household staff members told me how grateful they were that I stepped in to arrange things.

It made me feel like Barbra probably didn't treat them very well, and I was glad to have been here to help their holidays go a bit more smoothly, if nothing else. They were great people, and even though James probably paid them better than I ever got paid, they were normal folks like me who just made a great living serving others.

"Thanks, Marna..." I slipped out through the back door and stood on the veranda. I felt sad that I wasn't home with my family. They only lived on the other side of Green Bay, but James's party was demanding. I refused to let anyone else take this load on when he had paid me to do it, even when he offered to let me go. I could visit with Mom and Mimi tomorrow. Tonight was about him.

But I missed them, and I knew they were probably seated around the kitchen table doing a puzzle and watching a cheesy Christmas movie. So I pulled out my phone and called home just to hear Mom's voice.

"Ivy Sue!" Mom said with so much joy in her voice, it made me smile and made tears come to my eyes at the same time.

"Hey, Mom, how's everyone doing?" I pictured her sisters there too, probably smoking their cigarettes and filling the house with the stench, but Mom was too kind to ever send them away.

"Oh, you know... We're missing you. Did you get the packages we sent? Seems kind of fancy to be at an estate." She was silent for a moment, then I heard her shout, "Mimi, it's Ivy!"

"Hey, Ivy!" I heard my sister shout, and I chuckled and smiled. I missed her so much.

"I got them... Yeah, I'm only staying here while I coordinate the events. I'm looking for a place to rent when this is all done." Sadness washed over me again at the thought of living alone. I had never lived alone unless you considered living in a hotel for a few months "living alone". I moved in with Mike straight out of my parents' house and then in with James after the hotel.

Having a big, empty apartment to myself just didn't sound fun at all. I craved people around me, which was probably why I became an event planner to begin with.

"What's wrong, baby? You sound sad..." Mom sounded compassionate, but I wasn't about to tell her everything. She knew I broke up with Mike, though, so I leaned into that.

"Oh, you know... It's hard having a breakup during the holidays. That's all. And rebranding to an events planner and not just weddings is stressful. It's good, though. I know I can do it." My lips were sealed about the millions James gave me. If she knew that, she'd only think he was using his age, power, and money to manipulate me. And God forbid I tell her about the sex. I'd never hear the end of it then.

"Well, you just take one day at a time. And you can come home. You don't have to get your own place." Her offer was sweet but not going to happen. I wasn't going to live on the far western side of such a massive city and commute for more than an hour every day for work. Lover's Bay was much more likely to be the place I landed when all of this was said and done.

"Ms. Hart?" I heard, and I turned to see James standing in the doorway.

"Mom, I gotta go. I'll see you tomorrow." I felt sad letting her go, but duty called.

"Tomorrow, then. Love you," Mom said, and then she hung up, and I sucked in a breath and plastered a fake smile on my face.

"Let's go," I said, not sure why he'd come after me. "Is something wrong?" I followed James back into the kitchen. He shut the door behind me and offered me his elbow.

"Time to dance," he said, and I remembered the way he twirled me around that ballroom and our short but sweet dance on Thanksgiving. Thankfully, I hadn't had to do much more than that, but tonight, I wasn't feeling it. It really was weighing me down, not having someone to share the holidays with and having this massive growing ball of affection for someone who was so far out of my league it was comical.

I wanted to resist and tell him no, but I'd given him my word. He needed someone to dance with and he had already explained to his family, friends, and colleagues that it was customary for the host to offer a dance to any woman who was unattended. I just happened to be the only one unattended, and Barbra was nowhere in sight. I'd heard mumbling about that too, but no one was bold enough to come right out and ask.

So I let James sweep me back into his great room where the quartet played a soft stringed melody. He held me against his body as we swayed in time to the music. Everyone was dancing, not just us, and I felt a little at ease knowing no one was staring, but the ball of emotion, coupled with the growing, lingering nausea I felt, just never left.

I was exhausted and stressed out. I hadn't slept well in days. I'd been so hungry at times and at other times, I had no appetite at all, and the strangest thing happened when I smelled any fake scents—I got so sick to my stomach. A few times at night, I thought about that night in James's limo, but I'd done tests and they came back negative. I wasn't sure what to think.

"Ms. Hart, you seem down." James's soft whisper in my ear made goosebumps rise on my arm. I wanted to lean into his chest for comfort. My emotions were all over the place lately, and I didn't know why.

"I'm alright. I just miss my family." I forced a smile, and he reached into his pocket with one hand while he kept the other snugly in my back.

"I got you this," he said, and I looked down at the delicate snowflakes decorating the light blue wrapping paper. A silver ribbon had been tied around it, and the card was in the shape of a very sophisticated but animated reindeer. It brought tears to my eyes instantly.

"Oh, Mr. Carver. I didn't get you anything." I felt the warmth on my cheeks when I blinked out the tears, and he wiped them away with a thumb.

"I think you forgot. I asked you to call me James." His hand moved away from my face, and I flushed with embarrassment.

I wasn't like these people. Every single one of them wore jewelry that cost more than my parents' home. I had no education, no money. I had no car or even a home, and I suddenly felt very out of place, not just because he'd gotten me a gift and I couldn't return that sentiment. Hot tears burned my cheeks, and I walked away.

James followed me as I ducked into a hallway and sniffled, and he stood a few feet away as I stared down at the pretty paper and silver ribbon. "Why did you do this?" I asked, knowing he had spent a lot of time thinking about this. Even the paper and card were enough to make me swoon. He'd been studying my taste and hit the bullseye.

"I wanted to show you I'm grateful for your help and work for me." His eyes scanned my face thoughtfully, but that wasn't the answer I wanted to hear from him.

"Thank you," I said softly, and I wiped the tears from my eyes. "You'll have to excuse me now. I need to eat my dinner." I nodded at him and smiled. I didn't even know what was in this box, but I had a feeling I was going to bawl when I opened it.

"Yes, okay," he said, sounding a bit hurt, but he didn't stand in my way when I walked into the kitchen to get my plate of now-cold food. I took it to my room and locked the door. I had no other duties this evening, and I just wanted to be alone. More and more, I was beginning to believe I was going crazy. I hadn't felt like myself in days, and it scared me a little.

Maybe those tests were wrong and I really was pregnant. If that was the case, it would explain everything. I just didn't know how to feel if it was true. James Carver's baby? Inside me? How would I explain that without sounding like a gold digger?

19

JAMES

It hit me this evening, how lonely I'd be when the holidays were over and this house was empty. I let my guests finish their dancing and mingled with a few, talking and having another glass of champagne, but my mind was absent. I couldn't enjoy this party, even though it was Christmas. My thoughts were on Ms. Hart, who had all but disappeared from view.

The night started to wind down, and I showed each guest out individually. A few asked about Barbra, and I told them she wasn't able to make it. I didn't tell a single one I hadn't invited her or that she'd moved out, but I knew some of them were starting to gather the truth already. It wasn't official yet. The judge had to sign off and so did Barbra, and I wasn't going to make that announcement until they both did.

Fortunately for me, my friends and family were tactful. None of them brought up the elephant in the room, and we were all able to enjoy our Christmas party without heavy conversation or brooding emotions. For that, I was grateful.

When the last guest had left and the staff were busy cleaning things up, I found Marna in the kitchen running the dishwasher and stood in the doorway until she noticed me standing there. She looked up with a smile as always.

"Good evening, Mr. Carver. How did you enjoy the party? Ms. Hart did a wonderful job, didn't she?" The mention of her name made my heart pinch a little. She'd seemed so sad and upset when we spoke, and I was confused and a little hurt by her reaction to my gift, which she hadn't even opened in my presence.

"It was a wonderful evening." I smiled politely, but I hadn't come in here to discuss the night's events. I wanted to know where Ms. Hart was. "Marna, have you seen Ms. Hart? She was acting strange when I spoke with her. I wanted to talk to her."

Marna glanced around the kitchen then focused on her work again as she said, "No, sir. I thought she was acting down too. She didn't seem herself. I think she took her plate to her room to eat alone."

I nodded, understanding what she meant. Marna and I had been together a long time. She had a way of communicating things without really saying them. She knew I preferred to keep drama away from myself as much as possible, so she kept emotion out of her communication with me. But what she was really saying was that she was concerned too. Ivy hadn't been acting right.

"Thank you, Marna. You can take the day off tomorrow. Tell the rest of the staff too." I smiled. "Merry Christmas."

"Merry Christmas, Mr. Carver." She grinned and nodded, and I backed out of the kitchen and turned toward the bedrooms where I assumed Ivy had tucked herself away.

The house felt cold tonight, and not just because of the chill outside where a cold front was ushering in heavy snowfall. It wasn't just because I was realizing how lonely I'd be in this big place without Barbra here. It felt cold because I'd gotten used to spending my time with Ivy and she seemed distant. I was starting to think she was avoiding me, though I knew she was quite busy with finding her new office space and working with Mr. Sutter to do her business plan.

But even during our brief interactions, she seemed distracted, like her mind was on other things. Maybe I'd just read too much into it to begin with, but I'd thought we had a pretty good rapport. Though I had tried to warn myself that this could happen, that she'd realize it was a mistake to get involved with a man that much older than herself.

The closer I got to the bedrooms, the more I wanted to know what was happening. As I approached the room she was staying in, I slowed. I planned to knock and ask her if we could finally sit down and discuss what was going on between us, but I heard the faint sound of sniffling and then a cough. I wondered if she was feeling ill and maybe I'd been overthinking everything. Maybe she was sick.

I knocked softly and I heard the lock click. It was a bit discouraging that she'd locked the door, but she said, "Come in," so I turned the knob and pushed the door open.

Ivy sat on the edge of her bed with a pile of tissues wadded up on the bed beside her, and I realized she wasn't sick. Her eyes were red-rimmed and her nose was puffy from crying. She had her hands folded in her lap and her head hung.

"I just wanted to check on you." I glanced around the room as I stepped in and shut the door behind me. On the off chance that any of my staff walked by, I didn't want them to see her in this state. She'd obviously come and tucked herself away because she wanted to be alone, and I felt like I was already invading her privacy enough. "You were quiet tonight, and then you disappeared."

Ivy's shoulders bobbed and she looked up at me. "I'm sorry. I'm missing home, and well..." She sighed and picked up the pile of tissues and stood. "I got into a bickering match with Kevin who thinks I should be fighting Mike more. I just don't see the point."

I watched her walk toward the bathroom, and when she returned, her hands were empty, but her eyes were still sad.

"What do you want to do?" I asked her, because it was the most honest thing I could ask. This woman had been pushed around and told what to do by men her whole professional life. I didn't want to be that in her life too, especially since we had a no-strings-attached agreement. I really meant it.

"I want to move on. I just want to start over and not drag any of that drama into my future." She sank back onto the side of the bed, and I walked over to sit next to her. "And part of me is scared that it means Kevin has to go too. He got too comfortable with Mike's way of doing things. He thinks he is smarter than me, and he can't stand it when I want to make decisions for myself."

Ivy sat there looking defeated, and I couldn't stand it. Something inside me wanted to stand up to those idiots and make them leave her alone, though I knew the only way she'd ever feel confident on her own was to do that herself once and for all. But I could comfort her.

I put my arm around her in a friendly manner, rubbing her far shoulder, and she rested her head on my bicep.

"James, I'm really sad. Everything is difficult right now. I feel alone and..." Her voice trailed off, and she sighed.

"I feel the same way, Ms. Hart." It still felt strange calling her Ivy. I much preferred the sound of her surname, and she seemed to not mind it anymore. "But we both have to realize that the people in our past are in our past for a reason. Those ties weren't strong enough to sustain the relationships. We have to move on and make new ties, new relationships."

She wiped at her cheeks again and looked up at me, and our eyes met. It was a tender moment, not supposed to be sexual in any way, but the chemistry was always there between us. I wanted to comfort her and help her as she was moving on after her bad breakup the way she'd helped me when I thought I didn't need anyone's help.

"Ms. Hart," I said, thinking I was going to give her more inspiration or comfort, but she rose up and pressed her lips against mine.

"Things are chaotic right now, James. I'm struggling, and I'm not feeling like myself." Her eyes searched mine, and all I wanted to do was make her feel whole again. My eyes dropped to her lips and then back up to meet her eyes, and I noticed she did the same thing.

"It just takes time," I whispered, but she cut me off with a soft kiss.

Until this very second, my only intention had been to come in here and talk, but when she kissed me, it was hard to focus on anything but the way she made me feel. I deepened the kiss and found myself desperate to feel her against me again. As if whatever bond we shared had been fading and the relational battery was going dead, I needed a charge, and my lips drew the power from her so I could feel alive again.

I kissed her harder, cupping her cheek and biting her lower lip. "Ms. Hart, I don't think I can leave this room unless..." I let my words fade into the silence as she took hold of my tie and pulled me against herself so we would kiss again.

I had no control over my actions anymore as my hand slid down to her waist and found its way to the hem of her skirt. Slowly, I carefully slid it upward, revealing a pair of stockings that made my heart skip a beat. Her skin, so soft and warm against my fingertips, made my dick throb.

"Ms. Hart," I muttered between ragged breaths. "What are you doing to me?"

She smiled in a mischievous manner and said, "I'm simply giving you what you want." She guided my hand higher, urging me onward. "This is what you want, right?" I almost stopped right then and there. I didn't want her to think this was all I wanted, but I did want it. I wanted her. And by the look on her face, she wanted me too.

As if hypnotized, I obeyed her silent command, my fingers trembling with anticipation as they reached the lace-covered heat between her thighs. She moaned into my mouth, her body arching against mine, and I rubbed her through the soft, silky material. It wasn't enough. I needed more.

Taking a deep breath, I broke the kiss and looked into her eyes. "I don't know if this is such a good idea," I said, even though my actions betrayed my words.

"Neither do I," she breathed, her chest heaving against mine, "but it doesn't change the fact that I want you."

With that, she took matters into her own hands, literally, and unbuttoned my shirt. This was my last chance to walk away, to save us both from the consequences of our actions. Instead, I let her take control and allowed myself to drown in the moment.

She pushed me backward onto her bed and straddled my hips, draping herself across me until her tits were crushed against my chest. I held her by the hips and pulled her down onto my lap and she ground her pelvis against mine. She undid my tie and kissed down my chest. As she backed away, I slid the sweater up over her head and tossed it.

When she got to my fly, she was on her knees at the side of the bed. Her fingers nimbly undid the button and zipper, and my cock sprang free. She looked up at me through her lashes and smirked. She looked up at me, her eyes heavy with lust and need, and she tugged my slacks down. I kicked off my shoes as she pulled my slacks and boxers off, and as I backed across the bed, peeling my shirt off, she stood and removed her bra.

When her hands slid under her skirt and shimmied her panties down, I stroked myself and watched. She climbed on top of me and straddled my hips again, her skirt hiding both of our parts as she slid her moisture up and down my shaft. Her hands gripped my hip bones as she started grinding, and my God, I thought I'd lose it. I reached up and kneaded her tits, and she moaned softly before bending down to kiss me.

When I'd had enough of her teasing, I rolled us over and hovered over her. Her hand remained under her skirt touching her clit as I kissed her hard and crushed my lips against her mouth. She whimpered and wrapped her legs around my waist. I slid into her wet heat, sheathing myself inside her, and she moaned into my ear. I started to move slow at first, but her nails digging into my back incited me to pick up the pace. I pounded into her harder, and she moaned louder, her body arching off the bed. Her skirt rode up, revealing her shaven mound as I slammed into her again and again.

I didn't know how much longer I could last, but I wanted this to last forever. But she whimpered, "Condom," and I had to slow. I hadn't prepared for tonight. I didn't have one.

Her eyes searched my expression as I swallowed hard and tried to think of what to do. "Ivy, I…"

"Oh, God, I'm so close," she mewled, and I kept thrusting, gritting my teeth so I didn't come, and when her pussy clamped down around me, it took all my focus not to blow my load. She shook beneath me, shuddering and coming undone, and her pussy got so wet I thought maybe I had blown already, but the pressure in my dick was so intense I kept going.

"James," she panted, and I kissed her again and again, and when I felt my balls drawing up, I pulled out.

"What?" she gasped, and I flipped her over.

"God, you're sexy…" Her ass was on display, skirt flipped up over her back, and I used the moisture from her orgasm to lube her ass. When I pushed in, she grunted and gasped and clawed at the bed, but in seconds, I found a rhythm again.

"You feel so good," I panted in her ear.

"Oh, God, fuck me," she moaned, and I did just that. I fucked her harder than before. My dick slid in and out of her tight ass, and she screamed my name as her second orgasm hit her. Her pussy clenched, and I couldn't hold back any longer.

With a groan I came, and came, and came, filling her until my balls were empty and I collapsed on top of her. I rolled to the side and felt my dick still pulsing inside her. She was breathing heavily, panting, and I held her against my chest as I slid out.

She didn't move a muscle, and I kept my arms around her for a long time, kissing the back of her shoulder every now and then. And when I heard light snoring, I reached up and shut off the light, then pulled the covers over us. No way in hell was I leaving her now.

Something was going on, and we had to decide what it was. I couldn't keep pretending I wasn't falling for her.

20

IVY

When I woke to pee, I felt slightly nauseous, which made me feel nervous. James was in my bed, tangled around me. Not wanting to bother him, I carefully lifted his arm off my body and slid my legs out from under the blankets. I tiptoed to the bathroom and quietly shut the door, but my small pink makeup case caught my eye.

I'd taken a few pregnancy tests already, but none of them had come back positive. Still, my period was late, and it was unnerving me. I had a few more tests left, though I felt a little scared to take one again. I had felt nauseous a few times, though it was ludicrous for me to think it was even possible for it to be morning sickness so soon. But my nerves were shot too, so maybe that was what was causing the nausea and what made my period come late too.

I shivered as I pulled one of the tests out just to reassure myself and put these fears to bed. My clothes were strewn around the bedroom from my romp with James last night, and it was cold in here without clothes on. I sat on the toilet and opened the test and peed on the foam end of the little white stick. Then I set it on the counter while I finished up and washed my hands.

While I waited for the test to process, I slipped on my robe and perched on the edge of the bathtub. My bed called to me, but I knew I'd never get back to sleep now. When a few minutes passed, I picked up the test and looked at it, but in the faint light coming in through the window, I couldn't tell what the result was. So I flicked on the light and squinted as my eyes adjusted to the brightness.

There were two pink lines in the results window, but one was so faint I thought I was seeing things. My heart leapt up into my throat and I blinked several times to attempt to make my eyes work better, but no matter how many times I blinked, I saw the same thing—one dark line and one faint line, almost imperceptible. That sight made me want to vomit for real, but nothing came up.

I sat on the edge of the bathtub in complete shock for a moment. I had been such an idiot for not going to get the morning after pill when I feared the worst, and now it was too late. This test was telling me I was pregnant, and given how emotional I'd been feeling, even with my period only being a few days late now, I knew it was probably a fact.

I had gotten so excited and overwhelmed by the idea that James would invest in my company. Any thought of an unplanned pregnancy slipped my mind. Two million dollars was a lot of money, and that was all I could think about for days. I covered my face with my hands and stifled a sob as regret consumed me. I was so drunk that night, I didn't even remember the act of having sex with him, and now I was paying the consequences for that act.

My heart pounded and tears streamed down my face. I thought of all the things people would think of me when they found out I was pregnant and who the father was. James was lying in my bed after a night of sex yet again, and we still hadn't even spoken to each other about what was going on. We were both just out of really bad relationships, and everyone knows you don't just jump into something new right away.

People would take one look at me and think I was a gold digger, and they'd have proof of that too. Two million reasons I got pregnant and what James did to hide it. But how would I ever be able to hide it? I didn't want to raise a kid by myself, and I didn't want to marry someone out of obligation, which was what this would be. James was from the generation where if you knock a woman up, you marry her. But I wanted love—not an arrangement.

I heard a door shut, and it startled me. I swiped at my eyes quickly and grabbed some toilet paper to wipe my face and blow my nose. When I cracked the door open to see what was going on, I noticed that James was no longer in my bed, which made me sad and relieved at the same time. I didn't want him to ask why I was crying, though I wished he hadn't just snuck out like last night never happened. It told me everything I needed to know.

James wasn't actually interested in a relationship with me. He saw me as an investment, a cash cow he could hop on for a while to make more money. He was investing in my company because I was good at what I did and he believed that, but other than great sex, I didn't think he was interested in anything personal with me.

That made more tears well up as I scurried to the door and locked it, then I scrambled to get dressed and find my purse and phone. I scribbled a note for James letting him know I was visiting my mother for a while, and then I ordered an Uber to pick me up.

Mom and Mimi were expecting me later this afternoon, but when I arrived, it wasn't even eight in the morning yet. Mimi opened the door for me, and I followed her up the hallway. Her auburn curls had been swept up into a messy bun, but a few stray curls bounced at her neck.

"You're so early... What, did Mr. Fancy Estate kick you out?" she asked playfully, and I winced. The idea that James would ever ask me to leave felt painful. Of course, we'd made an agreement that I would finish planning the events and that my stay at his house was just until the Valentine's gala was over. But that still loomed six weeks into the future.

"Uh, I just missed you guys," I said, but I couldn't hide the emotion in my tone. I was glad when we walked into the kitchen to find that Mom wasn't up yet. My heart was so raw, I had to talk about this, and I wasn't sure I wanted Mom to know until I'd let it sink in a little more. But Mimi had been like my best friend growing up. I knew I could trust her.

She sat on the old wooden chair next to the tired table. It was a far cry from James's luxury, but it felt like home. I sank onto the chair across from her, and she narrowed her eyes at me.

"No coffee? What's wrong, Ivy?"

Before I could open my mouth to speak, my eyes welled up again and spilled over. I set my purse on the table between us, and when I put it down, Mimi grabbed my hand. Her fingers were warm from hugging her coffee mug, and mine were like ice from being outside.

"Hey, it's okay…" She glanced over her shoulder and then scooted her chair closer. The feet scraped on the old wood floors making a scratching sound, and her knee bumped mine, but she sat so close to me, she could put her arms around me.

"My God, I screwed up so bad, Mimi." I wondered if she could even understand me through my sobs, but she shushed me and patted my back. When she set her coffee mug next to my purse, I knew she knew this was serious.

"What happened? He didn't hurt you, did he?"

"God, no, nothing like that." I pulled away, and she reached into her T-shirt and pulled a tissue out of her bra, and I rolled my eyes and didn't stop my chuckle. "You still do that?"

"Hey, it's in case of emergency, and clearly, this is a sister emergency."

Mimi smiled, but she held my hand as I dabbed my eyes with the other. "So spill it, because I know that's why you came here."

I sighed and leaned back on the chair. It creaked under my weight, and I looked out the back window at the snow covering the back yard as I started talking.

"I'm pregnant, and before you say anything, no. It's not Mike's." I turned to look her in the eye, and she had confusion scrawled on her face.

"Whoa... First of all, you're pregnant?" Her voice quieted, and I nodded. Clearly, she understood the gravity of this situation. "But who?"

When she leaned in and waited, I confessed it all. The sex with James, his donation to my firm, the way I was falling for him, and then all my fears... "What if he thinks I got pregnant on purpose, Mimi? What if he thinks I'm just out for his money? Maybe I should give the two million back and move back here with Mom like she suggested."

More tears spilled from my eyes, and she got up to get the box of tissues from the living room. When she came back and sat down, I finally undid my coat and took it off. The chill from my body was going slowly, but my heart still felt ice-cold.

"Well, you could get a lot of money out of this if you wanted..." She plopped onto her chair and handed me the tissues, and I shook my head firmly.

"No, I don't want to. I don't want a penny of James's money. You didn't see the way his heart was so broken over his ex-wife leaving him. I couldn't do that to him." I'd rather take this secret to my grave than hurt him more. James had been through enough.

"Well, then keep it a secret for now. You know you have things left to do for this contract he's paid you for, so don't make that more miserable by bringing it up now. Give yourself time to think about what you want and how you feel. Do you love him?" she asked, and her eyes stayed fixed on my face.

I didn't know if I actually loved him or if this was just an infatuation. I knew what I didn't want, and that was some man telling me what to do. But what I did want was to make sure James was okay. To make sure I didn't hurt him worse or make his broken heart break more.

I stared at the back yard and watched a squirrel hop up a tree and thought about what Mimi said. Should I just keep this baby a secret for the time being? And what if James was upset that I kept it from him? It was only six weeks, but the burden of hiding something so huge would weigh on me. Still, if I told him and it caused problems, where would I go? I hadn't even found a place to live yet.

Besides, what if he really did decide that he had to marry me just because he knocked me up? I'd feel so much pressure to make him happy and not let him down, I might end up in a worse situation than I'd had with Mike. Why couldn't life be easy? Why did this have to happen to me?

21

JAMES

Sam sat across from me at my desk with a scowl on his face and his arms crossed over his chest. I'd been distracted again, staring out the window at the distant city skyline of Green Bay. I was thinking of Ivy and what she was doing. I knew she had plans to visit her family the day after Christmas, but she'd been gone two days now without a word. After the night we shared in her bed, she hadn't even said goodbye. Granted, I had slipped out to use the toilet while she was in her bathroom.

I came back to that note and I'd been missing her ever since. But at least her things were still at my place, and the party for Valentine's Day was still on. She had obligations to fulfill, so I tried to push away any negative thoughts and focus on the present. I just struggled.

"I don't get it," Sam said, shaking his head. The newly grown mustache on his upper lip seemed larger when he pursed his lips like that. "You're moody and distracted. I've asked you three times for the year-end reports, and you just stare out the window. What's going on?"

Sam wasn't just my friend or COO. He was like a brother. There was no hiding things from him, which was why he already knew almost every detail of my life. What he didn't know was Ivy Hart had invaded my world with her pep and charisma, and I was so infatuated with her that when she was away for even a short time, I felt like my world was incomplete, unlike Barbra who could leave for weeks at a time and I never skipped a beat.

"I signed the annulment." I felt the frustration clouding my mind, and it was the only way I could even begin to excuse my lack of focus or the mood I was in. Short of telling Sam everything, I had no other explanation.

"You've been done with her for months, James. Stop trying to pretend there's nothing going on. I get it. It's Christmas and New Year's, and you're lonely. I could set you up with someone. You need to get laid." He chuckled, and it was my turn to scowl.

"Thanks, but no thanks," I grumbled. I shut the file on the desk in front of me and ran a hand over my face. I had to get it together or I was going to snap at him, which was the last thing I wanted to do right now.

"So what gives? Is this divorce really messing you up that bad?" He drummed his fingers on my desk, and I stared out the window again.

It wasn't Barbra leaving or even Ivy being away. It was my lack of ability to communicate what I was actually feeling. I'd had a perfect opportunity to tell Ms. Hart I was falling for her and I let her drift off to sleep in my arms, and when I woke up, she was gone. Call it a lack of trust or fear of being hurt again. I just felt paralyzed whenever the idea of asking her to be with me came up. I was old, and she was never going to accept that.

"Come on, man. We're friends." Sam was waiting, and I felt like a ticking time bomb.

"I slept with her, Sam." My own shame felt suffocating. "The party planner..." He'd seen me with her at the Thanksgiving party and again a few days ago at the Christmas dinner at my home, though I thought we'd been very professional. I knew people were already talking about Barbra being absent, and my announcement at the Valentine's masquerade gala would likely not even surprise them. But this would.

"That teenager?" he asked, frowning at me.

"She's almost thirty. She's not a teenager." His accusation annoyed me, but I was prepared for it. It was probably what most people would think, anyway—that I was far too old for her.

"Okay, so she's an adult, but she could be your child." He scowled. "And you let her move into your home. What you have is a gold digger, my boy. You need to cut her off." He sat back with a smug expression, but he didn't know the first thing about her. My chest puffed up, instantly ready to defend her, but I wasn't going to sit here and argue with him.

"She's not a gold digger. She's a party planner, and because of all the events during the holiday season, I prepared a space for her in my house." His smug expression didn't soften at all. He just kept staring at me like I was a fool. Rather than continuing to defend myself, however, I just stood up. "I have a few things to tend to. We can finish this later."

"Look, man, I was just trying to protect you." Sam stood and smoothed his tie down the front of his chest and buttoned his coat. "I'll have Patsy ring you when I'm free this afternoon." He nodded and walked toward the elevator. He knew I wasn't going to sit around and talk trash about Ivy, and I was grateful that he understood my cues.

The instant he was in the elevator, I sat back down and called Ivy. I didn't want her to think I was checking on her, but I was. My world felt a little out of control not knowing what was happening. I should've just assumed she was only in this for sex and that she really was just visiting her family, but my heart wasn't okay with that assumption.

When the call rang through to voicemail, I left a message.

"Ms. Hart, it's James. I'm just calling to get an update on where we are for Valentine's Day. Did we decide to go with a dance floor? Give me a call, would you?" I hung up feeling defeated and put my phone back in my pocket. When it rang almost right away, I got excited, thinking it was her, but it was just my barber confirming my appointment later this afternoon.

I didn't know how long this visit of hers with her family was going to be, but I wished she'd just communicate. I wasn't good at it, though, so it stood to reason that maybe she wasn't either, and maybe I should be the first to break this ice between us and just tell her how I felt. If not, the next six weeks would fly by and she'd be gone, and I'd be alone.

22

IVY

I woke to the sound of bacon frying and Mom humming. The scent filled the air, making the entire house smell like the savory meat, which normally would be a horrible scent, but this morning, it made me ravenous. The way my stomach churned, though, I wasn't sure I could keep it down, but I would try. I was so hungry.

My body ached from sleeping on the sofa, but I pushed myself up and stretched away the stiffness in my muscles. Mom had been gracious enough to let me stay for the past week, and I had no way to pay her back. I should've been the one cooking her breakfast, but when I walked into the kitchen, I noticed Mimi standing by her side in front of the stove. They were laughing as they cooked breakfast, and neither of them saw me walk in.

I walked up behind them and rested my chin on my mom's shoulder. She glanced at me out of the corner of her eye as I wrapped one arm around her and one around Mimi and sighed.

"Smells so good," I told them, and Mom smiled.

"Good morning, how are you feeling?" she asked, and I was reluctant to tell her I was slightly nauseous. She knew about the baby—a hard conversation I'd been forced to have with her a few days ago, thanks to my loving sister who insisted I needed help.

"I'm okay," I said softly, but the way I turned inward in shame and anxiety over this new situation in my life had me drawing away. I wasn't really okay, but she knew that anyway. She was my mom. She could read me like a book.

"Have you thought any more about what you're going to say to Mr. Carver?" I hated hearing his name like that. It wasn't that Mom was judging him, but it made James seem cold or distant. I didn't want him to feel distant. I wanted so much more, and that made me feel conflicted for a lot of reasons. Not only was I having his baby, which he may or may not see as an attempt to get to his money, but for all I knew, we were having no-strings-attached sex as a fling and he wanted nothing more than to bed me and get money out of my company.

My chest physically ached when I thought of that. I hated that. Somewhere along the line, I sprouted feelings for this man, and that scared me. He wasn't exactly the one to open up and confess his feelings for me in return, if they even existed.

"No, Mom." I walked away and slumped onto a chair at the table, and Mimi brought me a plate with a stack of pancakes and a few slices of bacon on it. She set the syrup in front of me and offered a sympathetic expression. I wanted to be upset with her, but I couldn't. This wasn't her fault.

"Thank you," I whispered, and she winked at me.

"Well, you should tell him sooner rather than later, hon. The man has a financial obligation now."

I grimaced at her words and watched as she turned off the old stove and moved the pan of bacon from the heat. This place felt like it was straight out of the nineties with the yellow and orange linoleum and painted cabinets. I smiled as I remembered fond memories of childhood, but the memory soiled my mood as I thought of my own baby, still unborn, and how I'd even begin to offer them anything remotely similar to my upbringing.

"I just need time to process it, Mom." James had left me a voicemail asking about the party, but I chose to respond via a text message instead of calling. Everything was on track, and while I hadn't planned to stay here this long, I needed this break.

"Well, don't process it too long or he'll think he can get out of it. You know men these days." Mom carried her own plate of food and sat across from me. I didn't feel judged, but I did feel like she didn't fully understand how delicate this situation was. Yes, it was consensual sex, but it wasn't like I had tried to protect myself. I was too drunk to even care.

"You could always just stay here..." Mimi sat down next to me. She didn't even live here with Mom, but she was offering. She stayed here during the holidays in order to help Mom with all things Christmas and New Year's, but in a few days, she'd be going home. As it was, I had a party to finish.

"I can't..." I felt defeated. I had to return to James's house and finish the plans for the party or I wouldn't be upholding my end of the contract. I couldn't accept such a large investment into my new company and then drop the ball on my first job. It wasn't right.

"Let Kevin handle the party, Ivy. You need to put space between yourself and that man." Mom's stern eyes were narrowed in concern and warning, but I couldn't do what she was asking me to do. My job was important to me, and getting off on the wrong first step was a dangerous thing.

"Thank you, Mom, for being so concerned and caring about me, but I have to face this like an adult, not run and hide. It was as much my choice as it was his, and I just have to figure out a way to make it work."

The idea of having a baby at my age scared me to death. I wasn't married. I wasn't even financially secure, but giving up and letting life kick me in the teeth didn't sound like the right option. If I was ever going to be deserving of the title of "mother", I had to make hard choices and stick by my decisions. I had to return to James's house and finish everything for his Valentine's party... and somehow fess up that I was having his baby and pray that he didn't think I was a gold digger.

Mimi's plan, though, of keeping it a secret until after the final event was done, made sense. It wasn't like it was six months, just six more weeks. I'd be less than three months pregnant in total, and lots of women waited until later to announce their pregnancies—maybe not from their partners, but I wasn't sure if James would even want a baby, let alone a relationship.

"I have to go back," I told them. "I have a commitment, and I'm not a quitter. I'll figure out what to do about the baby later." I looked my mom square in the eye, and she nodded at me.

"I'm proud of you, sweetheart." She reached over and squeezed my hand. I accepted the gesture of compassion, but there wasn't much motivation on my part to feel proud of myself.

The only thing that could lift the weight on my shoulders was James's acceptance of this situation. Anything less would leave me feeling tortured.

23

JAMES

The second hand clicked rhythmically as time passed, and I stared at the glow of the Christmas tree in the corner of the room. The New Year's Eve event was going on at company headquarters, but I was at home sulking. The glass of whiskey in my hand couldn't comfort me the way it had so many times before when Barbra was away. This house was too quiet.

Ivy had sent me text-message updates letting me know she'd be back on the third, that Kevin was handling the NYE event, and that she was still in full swing for Valentine's Day, but she was being distant. It wasn't like we had a deep, intense connection anyway, but I could sense her pulling away.

Flames danced beyond the hearth in the firebox and caught my eye. It wasn't even a real fire with wood and smoke. Those flames were cheap and fake, just like my attempts at any relationship I tried. When it'd been Barbra in this house with me, I was the neglectful husband, choosing my company over her. Now that it was Ivy in this house, I felt overbearing, like I had smothered her or something.

What if the reason she was gone for so long had everything to do with the fact that my attempts to not make the same mistake I'd made with Barbra collided with Ivy's sense of newfound independence? What if I was overbearing before we even had a chance to see what might happen?

Scowling, I finished the strong drink and stood. I walked to the gas-burning fireplace and turned the gas valve off, effectively ending the ambience. The glowing tree annoyed me. I unplugged it, and I walked out of the living room, turning toward the bedrooms.

Ivy's room wasn't locked. Everything was exactly as she'd left it the day after Christmas. Her bed was unmade, clothing scattered here and there, and I stood in the doorway and surveyed it with a heavy heart. When she told me what true love really was—freedom, support, encouragement, selflessness... I felt so freed by that. I knew the tie I had to Barbra wasn't ever love, and that made my heart feel like I could breathe again, like I hadn't been a failure.

Now, however, as I backed out of Ivy's room and shut the light off and closed the door, it suffocated me. I'd let my heart come alive with her around. Our brief moments of intimacy aside, we'd really bonded. Dinners together, meetings, sharing car rides, every second was special to me, and it made me begin to appreciate and admire her for everything she was and everything she could do.

Now I missed her. I missed the smell of her perfume, the tinkle of her laughter. The way she never quite finished her meal and always had a bit too much wine. I missed the way she left her things lying around, but most of all, I missed her presence. I wanted her near me so I could make sure she was okay and happy.

I stopped by her workspace door and hovered for a moment. Any other time, I'd have just walked right in, but this door felt sacred to me. It represented a part of her that was so raw and vulnerable. Her attempt to start over in a new venture could be encapsulated in the square footage on the other side of this door. It was her springboard, her hope, her heart, and it was here under my roof where I could walk through it as if walking through her thoughts and feelings.

My hand tenderly touched the knob, and I made the decision to walk in. The light was off, so I flicked it on. The room lit up, and all I could see on every surface, including the bed, which normally served as a guest bed, were all sorts of decorations and craft materials. Thanksgiving turkeys lay next to Christmas bows and reindeer, and next to those were red and pink hearts. I smiled at the mess.

Then I walked over and picked up what appeared to be a centerpiece for the Valentine's gala. It was a heart-shaped candle with a wreath of red berries and twigs around it, and all seated on a silver platter. It looked like she still had dozens of these to assemble, but I couldn't imagine a more perfect decoration for this event. It was like Ivy walked through my mind and knew me well enough to know what perfection looked like to me.

The idea of that made me feel both happy and sad. In fact, I'd taken for granted how perfect every single event had been this year, far better than anything Barbra had planned. My ex-wife and I were nothing alike at all. We were about as opposite as a polar bear and a dragon. But Ivy and me?

This woman had studied me so well just by having dinner with me and learning my taste for culture and style that she'd practically taken scenes from my dreams and fantasies and woven them into a beautiful image I couldn't shake. I wondered when the last time was that anyone had done that for her, or if they'd ever done that. And then I wondered why I hadn't done that.

I set the decoration down and looked over a few more things before leaving the room just how I found it. My guilty heart knew I had failed her without her even saying a word. She wanted real love, the sort her ex had never given her, and I never thought to give it to her either, not truly.

I wanted to do anything and everything in my power to champion her and celebrate her, but I'd lacked the one thing I knew was essential—communication. Ivy deserved to know that I had fallen head over heels in love with her, even if she walked away and wanted nothing from me. That was the true definition of love anyway, right? To care about someone so much, you only want them to be happy and complete in life, even if it isn't with you? And though I had given her everything I thought she wanted, I never gave her the one thing she needed.

In my room, the swirl of alcohol in my head lulled me toward bed. I shed my clothing and left it on the floor the way Ivy would have if she were here, then I climbed into bed and lay down. I thought of the moment I'd asked her to dance with me at my events, most notably the Valentine Gala coming up, and it felt like a hundred years ago. So little time had actually passed, but in my heart, it felt like I'd always known her.

And when I closed my eyes and tried to sleep, the nagging thought that she might never want me due to my age tormented me. I tossed and turned and wished I could just sleep to shut my brain off.

But my father taught me to face my demons head on. The only way to win a fight was to fight it, not avoid it. So I made a plan to tell her that I loved her and let it be that. If she chose to reject that love, so be it. But I'd never know if I didn't try. And if I knew Ivy like I thought I did, the best place to do that would be at that Valentine's event.

After that, I'd leave it to fate.

When I finally made my decision, sleep came, and I dreamed of her. I just hoped she really did return and keep her promise to dance with me one more time. Even if it was our last dance.

24

IVY

My first day back on the job and I felt a bit anxious. I told James I would be back on the third, but I stayed another full week. When I arrived at his house on the tenth, he wasn't home—away on business, Marna told me. I was relieved. The morning sickness that started out as a slight annoyance had ramped up, just like I feared it would, though I found that avoiding greasy foods helped.

Now I stood next to Ginny and Craig, my first new employees for Event Queen, as they assembled more of the one-hundred-plus centerpieces I needed for James's Valentine's gala. It took roughly an hour per centerpiece, which was way longer than I had, considering I had to do backdrops and garland, and floral arrangements too. And it felt amazing to be able to hire people to work with me, though I did miss my old gang, which Mike poached.

"They're perfect, guys. You're doing so well." I smiled and rested my hand on Ginny's shoulder, and she glanced up at me in gratitude for my compliment. Her blonde hair was streaked with light blue in honor of the season of winter that had firmly gripped all of Wisconsin in its clutches. I thought it was nice.

"I'm so glad you like them... I'm so honored to be working with you, Ms. Hart." Ginny smiled, and I felt a pinch in my chest. Every time she or Craig said my name like that, I thought of James, who would never say my first name unless I forced him to.

I nodded and walked away before they could say any more, and I turned toward the back wall of the hotel ballroom. I'd taken measurements previously for the large tapestry that was coming, but I was still nervous. I'd ordered a hand-painted design from a local artist to represent James's company's reach in the area and what he's done for all of Lover's Bay and the greater Green Bay area with his innovation. Of course it was Valentine-themed too, so it would be appropriate, but I hoped it would touch his heart.

"So you'll be done on the thirteenth... That's one month and three days. Then what will you do?" Kevin folded his arms over his chest as he stopped beside me and stared at the wall with me. He'd seen my mood boards and the design I sent the artist, so he could probably assume what I was thinking. And after the arguments we'd had, I was shocked he even showed up to help me.

"Actually, I'm going to the event that night." I sighed and closed my eyes, trying harder to picture my plans and how they would look in reality. Usually, I was able to imagine things well, but lately, my emotions had clouded my inner eye.

"What? Why? We just send staffers to do that..." Kevin's eyes narrowed at me, and he pursed his lips and I knew what he was thinking. "So, will this be some new policy, or are you going to the event because of *him*?" His emphasis on the word "him" grated on my last nerve.

Kevin and I had been close friends for a long time, but he was overstepping his bounds all the time. I didn't always agree with him, and sometimes, I was willing to put him in his place to stand my ground, but I knew if I didn't learn to stand up for myself, I'd be plagued by men who thought they could control me for the rest of my life. If my best friend wasn't respectful enough to listen and support me, why would any man I date do that for me?

"I don't want to talk about this," I told him, and I turned and walked away. I headed toward the center of the room where the builders were erecting the wooden dance floor over the hotel's carpeting. It was an investment for my company, something that could be taken up and reused in other venues, and I was excited about it. It could offer me a greater reach when it came to more sophisticated parties and events. Kevin had voiced his dissent,, as usual.

"Well, we're going to talk about it. You can't think I'm just going to stand back and let you fling yourself at some man because you—"

I stopped suddenly and spun around with anger in my eyes. A few strands of hair fell from my bun and I swiped them out of my face as I cut him off. "You don't get to tell me what to do. You aren't 'letting me' do anything. I make my own choices. You are not Mike. You're not my partner. You're not even my business partner. You're supposed to be my friend, and right now, that's what I want. If you can't support my decisions, then maybe you can't be a part of my new company."

My heart hammered against my ribs. Telling him off was the last thing I wanted to do. I cared about him, and he really did have great ideas most of the time. And maybe I was just being too sensitive after what happened with Mike. Kevin had heard me complain over and over about how Mike was too controlling and didn't allow me to work as independently as I wanted to. When it was over, Kevin was the one who was there for me. Now he was acting like a stranger at times, and I felt lost. Or maybe I read too much into his attitude and snapped.

"Ivy..." he started, and he had a tone of concern, but I was just emotional, worked up over his attitude with me and hormonal from pregnancy.

The heater kicked on from the vent above me and dusted my face, making the heat in my cheeks worse. I looked away as tears burned at my eyes. Somehow, feeling my friendship with him crumbling was worse than feeling betrayed and controlled by my ex-boyfriend. Maybe because Kevin had been there by my side before Mike ever was, or maybe because he knew my heart in ways I never let Mike know me—ways I was already letting James know me.

That said something about these three men.

"I'm done, Kevin." My lip quivered as I spoke, and I blinked out more tears. "You watched Mike manhandle me and micromanage every choice I made. You saw him take and take and take from me, and you saw what it did to me. I can't take it from you too." I wiped away some tears, and he stepped forward to take my arms into his hands, but I backed away.

"I'm just saying, you are making bad choices, and it's not the ugly artwork you want for this party. It's your fucking heart I care about. You deserve better than to be some rich man's arm candy at an event so he can throw you away later on when no one is looking. He doesn't care about you, Ivy. You're on the rebound and you're dreaming too big. You're going to get hurt."

Kevin's words did something to my heart I never thought I'd feel.

It caused a shockwave that rippled through me and straight to my core, slicing through any hope I had that James could actually want me. I shook my head and backed away. It wasn't Kevin's fault he was speaking wise words to me, but the way they cut me so deeply made me angry with him. He could be nicer in the way he spoke to me, but that wasn't really his personality. Still, the emotion I felt made me reactive. It turned me into a monster I never wanted to be.

"Get out," I said softly, and I raised my arm and pointed at the door. My eyes never lost contact with his and he scoffed.

"So you're firing me? Or is this another tiff?" When he planted his hands on his hips indignantly, I wanted to change my mind and undo my words, but the look on his face egged me on.

"You're fired, and as far as I'm concerned, this friendship is over unless you can treat me with the respect I deserve. What you're saying may be true, but you don't have to be a total ass when you say things." More tears streamed down my cheeks as I thought of the baby growing inside me. Kevin had no idea, but I knew if he did, his tone would only get worse. He'd tell me I was an idiot for making that mistake and remind me how it was going to fuck up my new company, how hard I'd have to work.

Those weren't the things I needed my best friend to say, which only caused me to realize that Kevin was no true friend at all. Or if he was, he was just the wrong personality type to be able to truly be a friend to me now.

"Wow," he said, shaking his head. "So you're choosing a client over me? Because I told you you're getting too emotionally involved with him? Did you screw him too? Is that your new thing? You're sleeping with him so he gave you money? Do you know what that makes you?"

"Get out!" I shouted, and he shook his head one more time before he turned and walked away.

It wasn't Kevin's voice I heard. It was Mike's. I was right. Kevin had spent so long listening to the way Mike had treated me that he got lost in that sickening power a man can take over a woman. That wasn't my best friend, and if or when he ever snapped out of it, he had a long road to travel to get back into my good graces.

I watched him walk out and then I felt a soft touch on my arm and turned to see Craig standing there. "Are you okay?" he asked, and I saw how his jaw was clenched.

"Uh, yeah," I mumbled, wiping more tears off my cheeks.

"I thought he was gonna hurt you and I was totally gonna wail on him..." Craig's hands were balled up into fists, and I smiled sadly. It was a romantic gesture from someone who barely knew me. Though he didn't know the relationship dynamic between me and Kevin or why Kevin was being so over the top.

"I appreciate that, but I'm fine," I told him. "Go work. I'm going to wash my face." I offered another bittersweet smile and then turned and walked out of the ballroom toward the bathrooms.

As much fear and anxiety as I've had about telling James about the baby, and never once did I ever think he'd have treated me even half as bad as Kevin just had. My heart ached because I was losing people who were close to me little by little, and in exchange, all I had gotten was money for the hard work ahead of me and a new responsibility I didn't know how I would even manage. Kevin's words only made it worse, probably because I had that fear anyway, that James would think I'd gotten pregnant on purpose.

I was never trading sex for his money. It was never on my mind. The sex just happened organically because James and I were so alike. There was so much chemistry. It was why we could start a conversation before dinner that lasted well past dark and talk all the way until it was time to climb in bed and sleep. But I was a broke party planner, and he was a billionaire tech entrepreneur.

The chance of his seeing this baby as a good thing and wanting me for any reason other than as an investment was so slim, I'd sooner win the Power Ball. I didn't have a shot, and maybe I had just sent Kevin packing when I should've been listening to him. What had I done? What if I just sent my only friend away for good and James wanted nothing to do with me?

25

JAMES

Less than one month until Valentine's Day and the big event, and I was nervous. I checked the guest list almost every day, and today was no different. The RSVPs had been coming in daily now, and so far, there were only a few left to be returned, with every invitation boasting at least one "yes" and most of them adding a plus-one to their ticket.

In years past, this was normal, so this year was nothing out of the ordinary, except for the fact that Barbra wouldn't be there. Some of her friends, always on my list because they were friends of mine too, had given their positive response. I wondered how that would go over for them when I made my announcement that we were officially separated and our marriage had been annulled. I wondered what their reactions would be to that bit of news. But I couldn't let the potential negative reactions of a few people stop me from moving on with my life. By now, it was likely that Barbra herself had told them. That would definitely make my life easier.

I sat behind my desk agonizing over that guestlist for twenty minutes, but the real reason I was so nervous had nothing to do with Barbra or our mutual friends' reactions to our divorce. I was mostly on edge about my decision to tell Ms. Hart how I felt about her. With as distant as she'd been for the past few weeks since our sex on Christmas Day, I worried she would back out and not even attend the event.

When we made the contract back in August for her to plan this event for me, life was different for both of us. She made it clear that her part in the process was to plan the event and that she would have staff available at the event to help if needed. She never intended to come. But I'd asked her to come, and she'd accepted my invitation to dance.

Of course, when I first planned this, I thought Barbra and I had a fighting chance we never actually had. She had planned to walk away from me right before the holidays all along, or so it seemed. So my naïve hope that we'd have moved past all our differences and we could start over again with a renewal ceremony on Valentine's Day had been an illusion that faded faster than the dew on the grass on a spring morning. Evaporated.

Glancing at the clock, I knew I had a board meeting coming up, and before that happened, I wanted to check in. Ivy hadn't been joining me for dinner. She spent most of her time now at the ballroom, preparing decorations and whatnot. Most of my other events had been hosted at my home, which meant she was spending her days working there. But this one, being out of my home, took her away, though I was sure she didn't have to work past nine p.m. each night.

It felt like she was avoiding me, but I didn't know why. It was a bit discouraging, too, to think that all I wanted was to make her happy, but she constantly shied away. I didn't know what to think. I believed I was doing the right things, sending the right signals. I just hadn't come out and told her I wanted something more with her, which was my intention during the party. I wanted to believe it was something on her end, some stress I didn't know about, but my insecurities just pointed back to the fact that I was more than a decade older than her and she was probably way out of my league.

My eyes skimmed over the guestlist on the computer screen in front of me, and I drummed my fingers on my desk. If Sam knew what I was thinking about Ms. Hart right now, he'd lecture me. When he found out I was giving her two million dollars, he flipped out. I had to bicker with him for forty minutes over the intent, and when he finally got the point that I had been the one to bring it up and not her, he called me insane. He and Mr. Sutter were two peas in a pod, but it didn't deter me. I knew what I wanted, and she was it.

So I pulled out my phone and attempted to assuage my nagging worry by sending her a message.

James 11:48 AM: How are things going with the party planning and preparations? I'm looking forward to our dance that evening. Do you think you'll still make it?

I typed several more sentences but decided to delete them. I didn't want her to feel pressured at all, but I did want to remind her of her promise to dance with me. And I wanted her to know I was thinking of her and looking forward to that evening very much.

I expected it to take her a while to respond, and I was about to put my phone down when I noticed the words *Read at 11:48 a.m.* appear under my sent message. Then three dots popped up and scrolled across the bottom of my screen as she typed her reply.

Ivy 11:49 AM: Looking forward to it. We're halfway done with centerpieces and the ballroom is coming together. Can't wait for you to see it.

It wasn't out of the ordinary to get a friendly update like that from her, so I didn't read too much into it. At least I got a bit of relief that she was still planning to come to the event and accompany me during the dance. It knocked the edge off my insecurities to make them more manageable.

But the distance she'd put between us still gnawed away at me. I missed our conversations over dinner, and I wondered if she'd just grown bored of me or perhaps she realized that I wasn't what she wanted. It haunted me, and I wanted to draw her back in where I could get a feel for her. It might make me change my mind about revealing how in love I was with her at the event if I saw she didn't want me.

James 11:54 AM: Dinner has been quite lonely without you. Are you working late again tonight?

This time, the response was slower in coming and I almost gave up and stepped out to go to my meeting, but the moment I put my phone into my pocket, it chimed as she responded.

Ivy 11:56 AM: Gotta get this art done. I'm sorry. Another time?

Her response was a polite way of saying "No, thank you." I'd seen it before a lot, mostly in business, but I was accustomed to the polite decline of an invitation. But something in my heart just wouldn't let it go. It was like a craving for her presence that I had to sate or I'd go insane. So I sent another message.

James 11:56 AM: Okay, well Friday evening?

I hit *Send* just as the elevator chimed and Sam stepped off the elevator and into my office. "Time to go, buddy," he said, and I heard the excitement in his voice. We were doing a presentation with the board on a new prototype our team had come up with, and he was leading the charge on this one. All I had to do was be present, which was a good thing, given how distracted I'd been.

I glanced at my phone as I stood and saw the read receipt pop up under the message I sent. Ivy had read it, but there were no little dots indicating her typing a response. I followed Sam back to the elevator and down a floor to the board room, and still, there was no activity.

When the clock rolled over to the top of the hour and Sam started the meeting by announcing that lunch had been catered by a local restaurant and would be served after the presentation he was going to do, I locked my phone and turned it to silent mode. Even the best self-discipline couldn't keep me from checking my phone a dozen times during the meeting, but still no response. Ivy had left me on read, and that felt like a real rejection.

Maybe I was a fool for waiting until the party to tell her how I felt, or maybe it would just allow me to process the fact that she didn't reciprocate my feelings and help me let go of her gently. At least I'd have a month to tear her smile out of my mind before she was gone and off to new adventures. It would make the next several years of updates about her new company and its growth more bearable if I just let it go. Right now, I just couldn't. Not until she said with her own lips that she wasn't interested.

Then I could let my heart break again.

26

IVY

The wooden armchair situated next to the window was more uncomfortable than the bed where I'd started my scrolling in search of the perfect dress, but I had to force myself out of bed. If not, I'd have stayed there for hours, and that just seemed too depressing.

My thumb swiped upward, tugging the images on the page to move higher. The dress selection was fancy, but I'd never in my life been able to afford something like this. I just knew after James's other events and the dress he bought for me via Genevieve for going out to dinner, I had to look spectacular for this Valentine's gala in three weeks. Still, just seeing the price tag on some of these dresses felt like too much.

It was a business write off, for sure, but how could I justify twenty grand on a gown I'd wear once? The resale value wouldn't be nearly that much, and it wasn't like I catered to wealthy clientele who would require me to be in attendance at their events. But I couldn't very well just show up in one of my off-label business suits either, at least not if I intended to keep my promise to James and dance with him.

Anxiety over the whole thing niggled at my conscience. I wasn't going to tell him about the baby that night and ruin his evening, but I had decided to tell him the next morning as my things were being carried out to the new delivery van I bought with his money. Just the thought of telling him made me feel nauseous again, which was something I was getting used to feeling now. I swallowed down the bile and kept scrolling.

My heart just wasn't in this. Mom's warnings to keep James at arm's length and Mimi's jokes about milking this situation for as much money as possible made me worry about so many things. The James I'd gotten to know was a kind and warmhearted man. Using this baby to weasel my way into his fortune didn't sit right in my heart because it wasn't who I was as a person. Besides, I cared about him too, and I didn't want to hurt him at all.

My thumb kept scrolling, but now I wasn't even looking at the dresses. All I could think about was how bad it was going to hurt to move out of this place and how James would react to learning I was pregnant with his baby and I hadn't told him right away. It had to be obvious to him that I was avoiding him, though he'd have had no idea why. I didn't trust my own emotions to be stable, and if I broke down crying from guilt or shame, he'd ask why. Then I'd end up telling him and I'd have to live with that over my head for three more weeks.

My eyes fluttered up from the phone screen in my hand and toward the dresser where the fancy dress he bought me was lying. I could just wear that one to the gala, but it hadn't been cleaned. It would save me a bit of money, though the thought of what happened the night I wore it would plague me.

It already plagued me... But wearing that dress again and then dancing with him... I'd have a mental breakdown. I was in love with a man who was so far out of my league, he wouldn't ever look at me as an equal or as a partner. And his support of my new venture was strictly business too, so I couldn't even look at that and think he'd done it for personal reasons. I had to force my heart not to let my affection for him grow any more intense because in the end, it would be torn away anyway.

A knock on the door startled me and I stood up quickly. "Ms. Hart?" I heard, and I knew it was James. I jammed my phone into my jeans pocket and pushed the hair out of my eyes, then I walked over to the door and opened it.

"Hey," I said, standing in the doorway. I leaned on the partly open door and swallowed the anxiety I'd been feeling that all of a sudden felt like it was going to choke me.

"Hello," he said softly. The deep rumble of his baritone warmed me, though it shouldn't have. I scolded myself for feeling drawn to him, but I wanted comfort. "I thought we could discuss the party..." His eyes peered through the crack in the door over my head and then dropped back to my face. "Am I interrupting?"

"Uh..." I glanced over my shoulder at my messy room and felt embarrassed. Marna had come and helped me clean up a little, promising she'd do it all and I could just sit down, but I shooed her out and ended up leaving the rest there. It was messier now than it had ever been, and I was embarrassed. I turned back to him and sighed. "I was just looking for dresses online—for the gala."

His eyes sparkled as he smiled and said, "I could send Genevieve. She's really quite good."

"Uh, no, thank you. She's a horrible tart of a woman." My chest constricted as I remembered the way she treated me so roughly, but James's warm laughter relaxed me and I joined him with a chuckle.

"She is quite severe sometimes." He held out his elbow. "Come with me..."

I glanced into my room one more time, wishing I could climb back in bed and pretend I was sick or something. Then I sighed and followed him into the hall, taking his arm. "Where are we going?" I asked as I stared down at my feet with only socks.

"Well, Barbra had hundreds of thousands of dollars of dresses and suits. She just left and took almost nothing. You're a little shorter than her, but something in there has to fit. You can have your pick." James's hand wrapped around mine on his bicep. It was just the warmth I needed to reassure my heart—the very same heart I was actively lecturing to shut down and not feel.

"Are you sure she won't mind?" I tiptoed next to him as we approached his door, and he chuckled again.

"I paid for every single one of them, and she's gone. They're yours for the taking, Ms. Hart." He pushed open his bedroom door, and I let go of him as we walked into the cavernous room.

This time, with him here, it felt different. When Genevieve was with me, it felt like I was intruding, like I was seeing James secretly. But this time, I felt awkward and girlish, like a boy just invited me to his bedroom with naughty intentions. My cheeks flushed as he walked right to his walk-in closet and flung the doors open.

It was like a whole other room. I stood in the entrance and saw how large it was and gawked at it. On one side, rows of suits hung on hangers, at least twenty feet deep, and on the other side were gowns, dresses, and suits, color coordinated by the type of garment. Down the center was an island of sorts, a long white dresser with a glass top displaying the shoes organized within it. And at the far end was a vanity with a large oval mirror and lights, and on either side of it stood towering glass displays of every sort of jewelry imaginable. I felt overwhelmed.

"Here..." he said, turning toward the gowns. His hands tugged and sorted, sliding hangers back and forth until his eyebrows went up. "This one is the one I'm thinking of. Try it first and we'll see. If it doesn't work, we'll try any others you like."

James pulled a beautiful dark blue mermaid gown with gemstones sewn into the bodice. They looked like diamonds, but there was no way they could be. I felt my mouth drop as he smiled and held it up.

The halter neck had more of the precious gems, and a long, deep cutout between the breasts would leave nothing to the imagination.

"James," I whispered, feeling so overwhelmed there was no way I could even put that on, let alone wear it for his party. Barbra had to have looked amazing in it. I'd just be a poser, pretending to be wealthy when I was just a struggling party planner.

"Put it on, Ms. Hart." He held it out to me, and I took it, and the weight of it made me even more shocked.

"But this had to cost a fortune. It's silk Mikado." I knew it without even reading the tag. The material was used for couture dresses and wedding gowns, of which I'd seen dozens made. I looked up at him, and he winked at me.

"Only the best for you," he said, and he stepped out of the closet. "I'll wait here. Show me when you have it on."

I swallowed the lump in my throat as he shut the door and stared down at the dress. It said size four, which was my size, though the dress did seem long. With heels, it could possibly work, but what the hell was I thinking being in his walk-in closet, putting on his ex-wife's gown? Mom would kill me. Mimi would snicker like a fool, and Kevin would never speak to me again, if he ever wanted to, anyway.

But I stared at that gown a little longer and realized I actually wanted to. There was a part of me that just wanted to feel pampered and spoiled, and while I would never be the gold digger Mom feared James would think me, I did want to put this dress on for a moment and just pretend. Pretend that James loved me, that he knew I was having his baby, and that we were going to his gala together as a couple.

So I tugged my clothes off and put the gown on and stood in front of the mirror to examine myself. I was right. It was a bit on the long side, but it fit me perfectly. The dark blue only accented the warm tones in my hair, and I felt like a princess again, just like I had when Genevieve styled me.

"I'm waiting," I heard him call, and I felt my cheeks flushing with warmth as I thought of him sitting on his bed waiting for me. I almost started to cry too, because as much as my little fantasy made my heart feel hopeful, I knew it was a fool's dream.

I walked toward the door with the skirt dragging and opened both double doors at the same time. James really was seated on the foot of his bed. His eyes widened as I came into view, and then they darkened, flushed with desire. He was composed, though, trying to mask his real reaction, but I could see his pupils dilate.

"Well?" I said, stepping into his room.

"Turn," he said, and his voice was gravelly and choked.

I swallowed hard and turned slowly. The open back of this dress was lower than the one I'd worn before, and this time when I tried the fancy dress on, I hadn't kept my bra on. I felt exposed and chilly, and when he said, "Stop," I stopped. My back was toward him, and I heard the bed springs squeak as he stood.

His hands came around my arms, and I felt his hot breath down my back. I looked down at his right hand on my right arm and felt heat pooling low in my belly with his nearness.

"You look ravishing in that gown, Ms. Hart."

"Better than Barbra?" I asked, and I bit my lip, feeling stupid for saying that. Just the idea of comparing me to her felt wrong. She was a horrible woman for what she did to him, and I shouldn't have brought her up.

"Barbra never wore this gown…" His words vibrated across my skin. It felt like his lips were millimeters from touching my shoulder. "And I doubt she'd have looked as good as you, anyway. You make these diamonds look worthless." His lips pressed on my skin, and I shuddered.

"They're real?" I said, catching the glimmer of light that reflected off one of them. It made the dress seem that much more irrational. I couldn't wear this. I didn't belong in this world.

"And nothing compared to you..." He paused for a second, and his hand slid down my arm and cupped my hip. "Now, since you've got me all worked up, may I take this off you?" James pulled my body backward against his, and I felt his hard dick press into my ass cheek.

My heart was pounding so hard I thought it would beat out of my chest. He didn't wait for my answer, and I was glad. My groin instantly ached for his touch. His teeth sank into my skin as his other hand slid up to cup one of my breasts. I let out a breath of pleasure and arched my head back to rest on his shoulder.

"I'm beginning to think you brought me here just to fuck me," I told him, and while that niggling fear did weigh on me, I also didn't mind. He was incredible at fucking me, at making my body feel the heights of pleasure.

"And if I did, would that be so bad?" he asked, and I felt his teeth nip at the material of the dress. The snap at the back of my neck sprang loose, then the second one, and he pulled the front of the dress down.

It slid to the floor in a pool of fabric at my feet. I stepped out of the material, leaving me in nothing but my panties and socks.

"No," I breathed out, "it wouldn't be so bad at all." Before I could turn to face him, his hands were on me again, this time pulling me until he had me in his arms. He scooped me up and carried me to bed, and as we walked, I brought my lips to his. He kissed me eagerly, hungrily devouring me, and his stubble scraped across my skin.

James laid me down on the bed, his body hovering over mine. His tie draped over my breasts as he pulled his suit coat off. "Tell me you want this," he growled, and I knew what he meant. He meant was this wild sex okay, and was it okay if that was all it was? Part of me was okay with that because the arousal between my legs was demanding attention. But part of me wanted more. Part of me wanted this house and this life, and his love forever, and that was the part of me that answered him.

"I want this," I said. "All of it." Tears tried to well up, but he claimed my mouth again and I pulled him down hard for the kiss, crushing his lips against mine.

James worked to undress himself between kisses and touching. He had my panties and socks off in record time and was working on his trousers when I reached up and stopped him.

"Let me," I said, and he let out a shaky breath.

I unbuttoned his trousers, taking my time with each button until finally, they slid past his hips. His cock was already hard, ready for me. I grabbed it in my hand and started to stroke him. "You're so big," I said, marveling at the size of him. It would never get old.

"You're so tight," he groaned, and his head arched back when I licked him and drank in his precum. He tasted good, and I was ready for anything he was willing to do for me. I just hoped my heart would remember that this was just sex. Nothing more. Just sex.

27

JAMES

When Ivy said the words, "I want it all," my heart flipped. For all I knew, she was thinking this was just sex, and she was asking me to give her my dick as deep as I could push it. But in my heart, those words meant something so much more. I wished she meant "all" as in the life, the relationship—everything. And that was the only thing on my mind as I crushed my mouth against hers in a scorching kiss.

My hands trailed up her sides as I leaned her back on the bed again and nestled between her thighs. My dick rubbed through her moisture, but I only teased her with its tip as she hooked her heels around my back and offered me her entrance. She was a whimpering mess, clawing at my sides and panting heavily as she ground her pelvis against me. I was hungry for her. I wanted to enjoy this, to slow it down and savor every second of her.

I ran my fingertips along her collarbones and down to her hardened nipples, giving them a gentle squeeze before sliding lower. I dipped my head between her breasts and kissed the sensitive skin there, making my way down her stomach, tracing lazy patterns with my tongue. I needed to taste her. I needed to savor her.

"Oh, fuck," she moaned, her voice almost a whimper as my mouth closed in on her aching pussy. I could smell the intoxicating scent of her arousal, and it drove me wild. "Oh, God," she moaned as my tongue flicked at her clit, teasing the swollen bud. Her juices coated my face, and I lapped them up greedily, inhaling her sweet musk. I wanted all of her. Every drop.

One hand roamed up her back, gripping her hip roughly as I plunged two fingers inside her with the other. She arched her back off the bed with a gasp, and it spurred me on more. I suckled harder on her clit, working my fingers inside her in time with my tongue's movements. She petted my hair, tangling her fingers in it as my ministrations elicited tiny gasps of pleasure from her lips. When her pussy clenched around my digits, she whimpered and pulled my hair, and I knew she was enjoying it.

I continued to suckle and tongue her until she was quivering, thrusting her pelvis upward against my face. "Shit, James," she gasped, and her voice was frantic. "I'm so close…"

I couldn't help but smirk to myself. I wanted to be the one to give her the best orgasm she'd ever had. I wanted her to remember this day, remember me for the rest of her life. I wanted her to want more. I wanted her to mean it when she said, "I want it all."

"Mmm," I hummed against her core, and her pussy clamped down on my fingers. She grunted and arched up off the bed, curling around my head, which she squeezed tightly between her thighs. The rhythmic pulses of her hot walls pulsing around my finger made me smile, but I didn't stop sucking her. Ivy was exquisite, and I wished I could see her face while she was coming, but feeling the spasms and jolts of her muscles had to be enough this time.

Finally, her grip on my hair eased, and her body went limp underneath me. I kissed her thighs, then her belly button, then made my way back up to her lips. "I want it all, too," I whispered against her swollen lips. When I kissed her, she languidly searched my mouth with her tongue, drinking in her own moisture that lingered on my mouth and face.

"All of this?" she mewled as she spread her legs and rubbed her pussy over my hard shaft.

"Every fucking bit of it," I growled, and I ground my hips downward.

"My God, I want you in me." Ivy's hands pulled at my hips, and I gently guided my throbbing length to her slick entrance.

I felt the head of my cock brush against her, and I lost patience. Slowly was no longer an option. With one deep, powerful thrust, I plunged into her. Her walls enveloped me like a velvet vise grip, and the sensation was unreal. My cock slid into her with such ease thanks to her arousal. Ivy's nails dug into my back as she arched her hips upward to meet mine, urging me to go deeper.

"Oh, fuck," we both moaned in unison as our hips began to move in a primal rhythm. And in that moment, I knew I'd never wanted anything or anyone more than I wanted her. I wanted all of her, body and soul, and I was going to stop at nothing to make that a reality.

Ivy's hands came up to my face and held my head there as we kissed, and I gripped her hips and drove into her. Each long, deep thrust made her gasp and whine. It was music to my ears, a symphony she sang for only me, one I induced.

"James..." Her lips were frantic, kissing me and biting my lips. My balls were already drawing up. I chased release like a predator, and she was my prey. "Fuck... oh, fuck," she whimpered, and I felt her pussy tighten around me again.

"Come," I growled, and she choked out a gasp.

Her eyes rolled back, and she breathed through gritted teeth, and it was the sexiest expression on her face I'd seen her make. Her pussy contracted and pulsed, and I knew she was coming again, and the sensations pushed me over the edge. I exploded, spewing my seed into her and feeling it gush out around me, and as she continued to convulse, I kept the rhythm and kept her pleasure high.

When her body finally stilled, I collapsed by her side. We were both panting and sweaty. I never wanted to let her go. I realized now that more than anything, I wanted this woman by my side for the rest of my life.

My hand slid up over her belly and across to her hip. I hooked my fingers around her hip bone and pulled her against my chest. The sun was warm as it shone through the window onto her ivory skin, and I kissed her breast, then swirled my tongue around her nipple. It drew a smile to her lips and then a frown, and I reached up and tucked a strand of her hair around her ear.

"What is it?" I asked, and then I realized we hadn't used protection, and perhaps she was feeling uneasy about that. I wasn't afraid of any consequences that might lead to, though I would never purposefully try to cross her boundaries.

"James," she said softly as she stared up into my eyes, "there's something we should talk about."

Finally, we were here, alone with time. The lazy afternoon I hoped for was panning out perfectly, though maybe not exactly how I intended. I thought we'd talk about the party and then I'd invite her to dinner. We'd small talk or banter about common interests, and I'd allude to something more serious. My plan to tell her I was deeply in love with her at my Valentine's party hadn't changed. I still thought it was the perfect moment, but gauging her interest ahead of time still helped me feel more confident that I was doing the right thing.

And this moment between us, where she wanted to talk, felt like the perfect time to do some gentle prying. We kept finding ourselves like this—tangled in each other, sexually intimate, hungry for more. And we were ignoring the massive elephant in the room every time. But not this time.

"Of course," I told her, bringing my lips back to her breast. I pressed another kiss to her nipple and then cupped her other breast with my hand and kneaded it. She moaned softly and her legs, tangled in mine, tensed. When I licked her skin and sucked her nipple back into my mouth, she shuddered and pushed on my shoulder.

"James, please." She was resisting me, and I respected that. I could make love to her all day long if she let me, but she wanted to talk.

My phone started ringing, though, and the shrill of the ringtone made me scowl. "One second," I told her. I knew at any time, Sam would call me with problems, but I left things in his capable hands for a reason.

I leaned off the bed and dug through the pile of clothes to find my phone, lodged in my pants pocket. It was Sam, but he'd have to wait. I silenced the ringer and dropped the clothing to the floor, then returned to her side. Ivy was propped on one elbow with a pained expression.

"What is it?" I asked, and she sighed.

I tensed a little at seeing her face. She was torn up about something, though I didn't know what. I prepared myself for her to tell me this was just a fling or that she wasn't going to be at my party. I had no way of knowing what was bothering her, but my mind got carried away in the seconds that ticked by where she didn't speak. And then someone knocked on my door and I had to grit my teeth.

"Sir..." Marna called. "Sam is here. He says there is a work emergency." Marna's voice was barely audible, but it sucked the life out of me.

Ivy's eyes dropped in defeat and she sighed. I wasn't leaving until she told me whatever it was she needed to say.

"What is it? Work can wait." I realized in that instant that had I made this sacrifice for Barbra the way I was for Ivy, my life would've been entirely different. But here I was, trying my hardest for a woman whose affections remained a mystery to me.

"I, uh..." She smiled politely, and I knew what she was about to say was most definitely not what she had intended to talk about. "We won't see each other much for the next few weeks. I'll be pulling long days every day at the ballroom. So the next time we see each other will probably be the day of."

Her words hit me like a kick to the chest, but they weren't a death blow. She was still planning to go to the event, and that was a good thing. I just wished she wouldn't keep hiding from me. There was no way she needed that much time to do this work. The moment I opened my mouth to express that, however, I became like Mike. I couldn't do that. I wouldn't micromanage her time or affection. It had to be her choice.

"Of course," I said, capturing her hand and bringing it up to my lips to kiss her knuckles. "And I look forward to seeing you in that dress again, next time, for a dance."

"Sir! Sam is here!" Marna shouted, and I knew if I didn't pull myself away from Ms. Hart now, Sam would barge in here and embarrass her.

I reluctantly slid off the bed and shouted, "Coming!" Then I dressed as quickly as I could, stole one more kiss from Ivy, who still lay in my bed, and stepped out of the room.

My mind was reeling over that interaction. The sex was incredible as always, but her words haunted me. There was no way I could know what she wanted to talk to me about, but it seemed serious enough to affect her emotions, which meant it was probably not about a party. It was probably personal. And if it was personal, it was either good news or bad news.

So why did my mind immediately go to the worst-case scenario and fear she was going to tell me she didn't want whatever this was, this undefined thing we had going on that kept sucking us in? And what if she was going to end things? Would I even survive that?

28

IVY

My stomach churned and woke me up. It wasn't the first time morning sickness hit me before my alarm went off and it wouldn't be the last. But I stayed tucked away under the covers where it was warm, staring at the first fingers of light creeping up on the horizon out my window.

Each morning I woke up and felt sick, I reminded myself of the countdown I was doing in my head. Twenty-three days until the party. That meant twenty-three days until the torture of keeping this secret was over. I'd almost spilled it last week when James and I had sex in his room. I had been so close to telling him, and we got interrupted. It was on the tip of my tongue, ready to march right out into the open and unburden me, and I wished I'd have just blurted it out.

The weight of it was so heavy, if I didn't continuously keep myself busy with work or apartment shopping, I'd start crying. I had packed my schedule so full of activities, I left James's house at dawn daily and came back well into the night hours. He waited up for me one evening, but he'd fallen asleep on the couch in his living room. I didn't bother him, though I did hear his bedroom door shut when he finally turned in an hour later.

I hated that I had to put this space between us, but things were getting too real. I knew that the instant I let those words slip from my mouth during sex. It was a huge mistake that could've turned out badly. Luckily, he thought I meant all of him, as in the sex, his dick, an orgasm. The sex was fantastic too, like he poured himself into it more than any other time, but that's all it was. He proved that when he leapt out of bed and rushed off to work.

Though, if I told him that—that he'd failed by running out so quickly—I would've been no better than his ex-wife. I never wanted him to think I was a nag who couldn't be alone. Independence was my chief cornerstone after dealing with Mike and his controlling behavior. But that didn't mean I wanted to deal with the issue completely by myself, and James was addicted to his job. I didn't want to end up like Barbra, being neglected, either.

Sighing, I rolled over and pulled the blanket up around me and heard my phone vibrate. I had sent Mimi a text late last night when I heard James slip into his bedroom. My conscience was so tormented by the fact that I was living under his roof, enjoying the benefits of everything he offered, and yet I was lying to him. What was supposed to be just sex wasn't. I was helplessly in love, and the tiny baby growing inside me was a result of that insane affection.

I reached for my phone to see I was right. Mimi had texted me in response to my desperate plea for advice. Mom insisted that I tell him right away, which I was actually leaning toward doing, but Mimi's stance seemed logical too.

Mimi 7:04 AM: Girl, you're nuts. Don't tell him. If he's happy, great. But what if he freaks out?

I frowned as I imagined James getting really upset with me over this. If he thought for even one second that I planned this, his mind would instantly go to one thought—I was a gold digger. And he'd hate me. I'd go from being the woman he wanted to fuck to the woman he wanted to hate.

Ivy 7:05 AM: But I'm lying to him. I feel so guilty.

I sent a frowning emoji to her and felt tears welling up. Mimi didn't understand how bad this was tearing me up. My phone made a swooshing sound as she responded.

Mimi 7:05 AM: And if he's angry about it when you tell him, it means you either have to live with an angry man and deal with that stress or you're instantly homeless.

I thought of the apartments I'd looked at over the past few days and knew nothing was within my price range. I would have to look further out into the suburbs, which meant a longer commute. That or I'd have to move home with Mom. So I had twenty-three days until I was homeless. That was what it amounted to.

I didn't respond to her because I knew she was right. I locked my phone and dropped it on the nightstand as my fear and guilt ate away at me. I wanted to tell him, and not so I could unburden myself but because I wanted to tell him I loved him. It just seemed like if I was going to drop bombs, I should drop them all at once. That way, my heart would only have to feel the rejection once.

I tiptoed to my shower and turned on the steamy water and let it fog up the bathroom before I stepped in and under the hot flow. My thoughts were never going to get any clearer until this secret was out, and if I didn't get a grip and focus, I wasn't going to do my best work for James. And I also risked making bad choices for my future when it came to my store front and my new home.

As much as I agreed with Mimi and knew she was speaking wisdom, I knew in my heart that I had to tell him. I decided that if he was in his room when I left, I was going to say something. If not, I would take it as the universe's way of telling me my sister was right. So in the interest of getting this off my chest and knowing once and for all whether he wanted me or not, I hurried.

I finished my shower in record time and neglected the hair dryer. With still-dripping ringlets moistening my suit coat, I shoved my feet into my shoes and grabbed my purse and phone. The delivery van was outside, probably covered in ice or frost, so if this turned out badly, I didn't have to wait for an Uber driver. I could just jump right into the van and get out of here. And with one last deep breath to bolster my confidence, I stepped into the hallway and walked toward his door.

It was ajar, which wasn't a good sign, and when I knocked on it, Marna appeared and opened it from inside.

"Morning, Ms. Hart. Mr. Carver is gone already. Left about ten minutes ago. What can I do for you?" Her cheery smile made my heart sink. I knew it was reflected on my face as tears welled up in my eyes and I frowned.

"Ten minutes?" I repeated numbly.

"Yes, ma'am, he had an important meeting this morning. Is something the matter?" Marna took a step toward me and reached for my hand, but I backed away.

"No, nothing." I swiped at my eyes and smiled. "I'll be off to work now." I backed away and turned toward the front of the house, but the hot tears wouldn't stop. I knew I was just hormonal and that eventually the waterworks would stop and I wouldn't cry as much, but right now, I needed this cry.

I schlumped out to my new van and started it. It felt like even the universe was conspiring against me to keep me from telling him. I had so many chances, but I was so afraid he was going to react badly and push me away entirely. Now I just didn't care. My tortured mind needed rest, and telling him was the only way to get that rest. I even thought of writing a letter and leaving it on his pillow, but it seemed too impersonal, and I'd never be able to look him in the eye again.

When my phone buzzed, I figured it was Mimi, and I was right. I pulled my phone out of my purse and read her message.

Mimi 7:39 AM: So you're not telling him, right? Don't be an idiot, Ivy.

I responded with a heavy heart, much to her chagrin.

Ivy 7:40 AM: I'm not telling him. Okay?

Then I sent another text.

Ivy 7:41 AM: But I need your help. Kevin isn't speaking with me right now, and I need someone I trust to help me with this party. Plus, I might need emotional support. Can you come stay the week of Valentine's Day and work for me?

I sent a crying face emoji and waited for her response. It was a single thumbs-up and I knew it meant she was in. Now if I could just survive the guilt until then, it would be over.

Twenty-three days. That was all I had left.

29

JAMES

The rain and clouds hovering over Lover's Bay made the view from my office windows gloomy. I'd been in such a sour mood for days, and beating myself up over it wasn't helping. I stood with my hands in my pockets staring out across the city with a lump in my gut. When ivy told me she would be busy working, I assumed she would end up working some of those days from the workspace in my home, and I was right.

Today was one of those days, and I knew she was at my house putting some of her creations together. I'd seen her team coming in this morning when I was on my way out, and my heart felt torn. I wanted to be there with her, but after Sam's interruption a few weeks ago when I was in the afterglow of sex with Ivy, things at the office had blown up in a good way.

Our shareholders were awaiting news from the new microchips we were in development on, and I was so busy trying to keep things running smoothly, I had barely sat down. In the past when this happened, I just dug in and did the work. But those days were days when Barbra was the one at home, and I justified every decision as if work were the thing I had to prioritize, which I knew now was a mistake.

I had let my passion for my company cloud my judgement, which was very much not cloudy anymore. I didn't want to spend my days at this office working fourteen hours and being too exhausted to think when I got home. I wanted to have time for my life, and I wanted that life to be Ivy. But here I was doing the same thing to her that I'd done to Barbra, and all before I even asked her to commit to me. It didn't bode well for a relationship if I couldn't even change my habits.

"You're moody again. What crawled up your ass?" Sam cracked open a soda and walked over to stand next to me. I avoided eye contact, though through his reflection, I could see he was staring at me.

"We're working too much. How does your wife not care?" I scowled at my own reflection in the window and wondered if Sam's relationship was on the rocks the way mine with Barbra had been for years.

"Ah, she'll get over it. I buy her everything she wants." He chuckled and slurped from the soda can and then cleared his throat. "So you're just overworked? This is new…"

Sam had a point. It wasn't like me to feel the pull of something more strongly than my passion to grow this company. I believed in the advancements we were making. We were on the cutting edge and staying ahead of the game. But my heart longed for Ms. Hart and to tell her how I felt. It consumed my thoughts and made me distracted and grumpy.

"I'm going home," I told him, and I turned and walked to my desk. "You'll have to do the meetings without me." I glanced at the time on my watch and saw that it was just midday, but I'd had enough. As CEO, I deserved a day off, even if it meant shirking a few responsibilities.

The idea of surprising Ivy with a cup of coffee and some good conversation put a smile back on my face for the first time today, and I took out my wallet, keys, and phone, and looked up at Sam who was scowling now.

"You can't do that. What will the board think if you just walk out? This is critical. We're dancing around deadlines like crazy and—"

"You heard me," I told him firmly. "I'll be in tomorrow. Just hold down the fort." I walked past him with his scowling face and stepped onto the elevator and pushed the *Close Door* button.

The new lightness in my chest carried me to my car. I felt like I was floating on air as I climbed in and my driver ushered me home. I wasn't going to tell her yet. My plan was still intact, but seeing her face and hearing her laughter was something I deeply craved. I wasn't pleased with the idea of not seeing her for days or weeks on end. I knew now why Barbra had gotten so lonely. It was agonizing.

In fact, I was so enthralled with the idea of seeing her, I forgot entirely to stop and pick up that coffee, which was a good thing. Her delivery van wasn't out front when we pulled up, and when I walked to her workspace and she wasn't there, I realized I'd have had to drink that coffee myself.

The way my heart and hope deflated at the sight of the dark, empty room was only further proof that I was madly in love with Ms. Ivy Hart, and if she didn't reciprocate my affection when I confessed it, I was going to be in for a world of hurt.

30

IVY

With only four days left until the event and time ticking down, I had Mimi come to town even earlier than planned. Her original idea was to come on the thirteenth to help with final last-minute things, but without Kevin on board right now, I needed more help sooner. I could've just hired someone, but my heart was really messed up and confused right now, and having Mimi near me was an added level of comfort.

She hefted a crate of Christmas decorations toward the door, visibly straining from the weight. I stared at the plastic crate in her hands and watched as she walked past, and my eyes teared up a little seeing the Christmas centerpieces I had worked so hard on. They had been so beautiful on James's tables at his party, and when he told me I could keep them to repurpose or reuse them, I knew I wanted one to keep just for myself.

I stood there staring after Mimi as she continued to help carry things out to the delivery van. Four days to event time meant four days until I had to be out of here too, with all of my belongings. I had to leave this place empty, which made my heart feel empty too. I didn't want to leave this all behind, and it wasn't for the luxury of it. It was because I'd fallen deeply in love with James and the idea that we would have a baby together.

The thought of raising this baby alone scared me, but I knew I could do it. And the longer I adjusted to the idea, the more I liked the thought of having a little one to love me and shower in my affection. So the fairy tale my brain and heart had concocted—one where James fell for me and swept me off my feet like I was a princess—seemed so absurd and far away. The pragmatic reality that he might never look my way again after I told him was the cold truth, and I had to keep that in mind too.

When Mimi walked back in, I was still standing in the same place I'd been when she walked out. I zoned out, staring at the stack of crates left to be put into the delivery van to be hauled to my storage unit. The new storefront was being prepped and renovated and wouldn't be available until the first of March, so in the interim, it meant I was transient.

"What's wrong with you?" she asked, nudging me with her elbow as she turned to look at the crates. "None of them are going to fit. This load is full. We'll have to tackle it in the morning." Mimi raised her arm and looked at her watch and tapped the face of it. "It's too late and I'm getting tired."

"Tired," I repeated, still zoned out. It didn't feel right moving all this stuff out. This place had become my home since I moved in back in November, more so than that hotel room. It felt like the only thing that tethered me to who I used to be, and with a new company, new building, new life, I felt like I lost part of myself. But I felt like with James, I'd found a part of me I didn't know was in there.

"Ivy," Mimi said, snapping her fingers in front of my face. "Hello…"

I blinked and turned to look at her eyes. She seemed concerned, her forehead furrowed. She rested a hand on my shoulder and shook her head. "Are you okay?" The way her nose scrunched and she cocked her head, I knew what she was thinking. "Did he reject you? Is that why you're so off? You told him about the baby and he shot you down..."

"No, nothing like that," I said, feeling tears streak down my cheeks. I swiped them away and turned away from her as shame warmed me from head to toe.

"Then what?" Mimi got her manhandling skills from Mom, who always made us face her when we were talking. She gripped me by the shoulders and forced me to turn around. "What happened?"

My lip quivered, and I blinked out a few more tears. Leaving this place felt like leaving him, and it was breaking my heart. I hadn't even told him the truth to even know if he would react poorly, but my heart had it settled. He didn't want me.

"Oh, God, no..." She rolled her eyes and her head rocked on her shoulders. "Come here," she said as she pulled me in for a hug. Her arms wrapped around me tightly, and she shushed me as she rubbed her hands up and down my back. The thick sweater I picked to wear today was scratchy against my skin as she did that. "You're in love, aren't you?"

I sobbed into her shoulder and nodded, and she continued to soothe me for a second. "I don't know what happened, Meems. I just don't want to tell him now..."

"Hey, shh..." Her hand rubbed and rubbed, but eventually, she pulled me away and held me at arm's length with a stern but compassionate look in her eye. "Why don't you want to tell him?"

I sucked in a breath and wiped my cheeks again as I tried to compose myself. "Well, I mean... I tried to tell him. We had this moment, but it got interrupted. And now I just... I don't want to tell him because what if he hates the fact that I'm pregnant and sends me away? What if it ends everything?"

My head dropped, and she shook me gently by the shoulders. "Then we'll be the most badass mom and aunt who ever lived, and you'll find a prince charming to sweep you off your feet for real. If he is too big of a douche to see how incredible you are, he doesn't deserve you." Her words pricked my heart because I knew they were true.

If Mike had turned me away, I'd have told him to fuck off. But the thought of James saying that to me made me feel terrified. I raised my chin and looked her in the eye, and she sighed.

"Let's have a snack and watch a movie, okay?" she asked, and her head dipped.

"Yeah, okay..." I gestured at the hallway. I left Mimi in her bedroom and moved toward the kitchen where I had Marna set out a charcuterie board and a bottle of sparkling grape juice for us tonight. She had insisted that she stay and cook us a proper meal, but I told her the snack would be fine. And now after that emotional meltdown, I wasn't even hungry.

When I was on my return trip from the kitchen, I noticed James in the living room and lingered by the door for a few seconds, just long enough for him to see me and stand up.

"Ms. Hart..." He looked surprised but calm. His lips curled into a soft smile and he held up a glass of wine. "Care to join me? I was just thinking of you..."

The chemistry was there. I was drawn to him, but the idea of sitting down with him, even for a second, made me feel nauseous. I'd cave. I would blurt out the truth and get emotional again, and everything would end tonight. I swallowed hard and shook my head. I wasn't ready for it to end tonight. I wanted that dance on Valentine's Day.

"Uh, no, actually...." I looked down at the snack in my hands and back up to his face. "My sister is here. We worked late. Just having a snack before we nod off. Have a lot to get done still." I had told him we wouldn't see each other until the event, and I thought that would be the case. This incidental run-in was not supposed to happen.

"I see. She could join us too." I wondered about the pinch of disappointment I saw in his eyes, but I didn't say anything.

"We're really tired," I said, lying. I wasn't going to sleep again for a month. I was too anxious.

"Tomorrow, then…" he said, sounding hopeful, but I backed away into the darkness.

"Goodnight, James."

I walked back to my room with heaviness in every step and tears welling up again. Four more days of this torture, then a magical dance at his party. And then it was over and my heart could heal. A man like him deserved someone very different from me, even if it was just sex he wanted. I was no good for him.

31

JAMES

The rap on my door caught my attention, and I turned and said, "Come in." I didn't know why I hoped it would be Ms. Hart, but I did. I hoped she had one final thing to say or do before leaving for the event gala, though I didn't even know whether she was still here. So my heart sank when the door swung open and it was Marna.

"Sir, Sam is here," she said with a nod, and she backed away with a smile as Sam took her place on the threshold and walked in.

"Hey, now there's an overdressed man puttin' on the Ritz for a bummer of a party..." He chuckled as his eyes swept down over my expensive tuxedo to my Armani shoes. I'd told him exactly why this party was still going on. On top of the fact that I was finally making a statement about my divorce—even to a few members of the press who would be in attendance by invitation—I'd be making another precious announcement to all of my friends.

The fact that this gala happened every year was just a triviality to me this year. Tradition meant nothing without those with whom you hold it, and if tonight worked in my favor, I'd have a whole host of new traditions to make with Ms. Hart. If not, I might let them all slip right off my agenda and become a recluse.

"You can never be overdressed. The outside reflects the inside," I told him, winking. Nothing was going to get me down today, not even jibes from my closest friend. Today was the day I got to tell the woman of my dreams that I was in love with her in front of an audience of my peers.

Sam shut the door and walked farther into my room and whistled through his teeth as he moved. He, himself, was dressed to the nines as well. I assumed everyone in attendance this evening would be. It was the biggest gala of the year in this area. Only the most elite were invited. That just made it all the more exciting and anticipatory for me. Ivy would be honored in front of all those people in such a dramatic fashion, I couldn't wipe the smirk off my face just thinking of her reaction.

"You really have it bad for this girl, huh?"

I hadn't really told Sam about the intensity between me and Ms. Hart, but the way we interacted around the subject of her in conversation probably told him everything he needed to know. She'd been on my tongue day and night for weeks. She was all I could think about, and it came out in my words and body language. I turned back to the mirror in front of which I was standing and continued to tie my bowtie.

"I'm in love, Sam… And before you lecture me—keep it to yourself." I eyed him through the reflection. "I am wise enough to know what I'm getting into. I just hope Barbra doesn't make it a big deal."

Wisely, Sam avoided that topic as well, and he changed the subject. "I heard Cameron Sullivan is performing?" His eyebrows rose in curiosity, and I smiled, thankful that my friend understood my stance and by his silence on the subject showed his support.

I turned with a smile and nodded at him, and we delved into the details as I put on my cufflinks and shoes and we headed down to my car. Sam's wife waited in the living room for him, and together, the three of us climbed into my limo and were off to the venue.

When we walked into the ballroom, I was blown away. Barbra's previous Valentine's parties were mediocre compared to the punch of Ms. Hart's designs. The room was full of reds and pinks—roses in vases on every table, velvet curtains draped along the walls, and little twinkle lights strung above us like stars. In the center of the room, the dance floor was packed with couples, all gliding smoothly to the music. The live band played soft tunes, the kind that made everyone sway in time, their feet barely touching the ground.

Along one wall, a massive chocolate fountain stood bubbling with rich, dark chocolate. People crowded around, dipping strawberries, marshmallows, and even little heart-shaped cookies into the flow, their laughter and chatter filling the air. Near the fountain, there was a hand-painted tapestry splashed in reds, pinks, and whites, with swirling patterns that seemed almost alive. It was huge, covering the entire wall, and it pulled the whole room together, like it was telling a love story without a single word.

Sam whistled through his teeth again and his eyes went wide. "Sheesh, she makes Barbra look like a fool, doesn't she?" he said, and his wife patted his arm.

"I need chocolate, dear," she told him, and she pulled him away from me as I chuckled at his response. I watched them weave through the crowd toward the fountain on the far wall and focused my eyes on the dancefloor where I knew tonight the magic would really happen. I couldn't wait to tell her I was in love, but more so, I couldn't wait to rub elbows with every single person here and tell them how incredible she was.

This entire event couldn't have been more perfect so far. I hardly had to do a thing. Just showing up and seeing the decorations, hearing the band, I knew every one of my friends and colleagues would be as amazed and awestruck as I was. The work spoke for itself. I couldn't wait to see her now…

3 2

IVY

With the heels on the dress wasn't quite as long, but it was heavy. I bustled about with orders for servers, musicians, the bartender, and even the chef in the kitchen. The hotel staff flitted about too, dressed in their most dapper attire, and I felt like a queen.

Mimi had tied my hair up into some twisted mess on my head with pins and ribbons, and while I would never have done it to myself, I thought it was beautiful. If I weren't wearing a million dollars on my body, I'd have thought the up-do was a bit much, especially when she pinned the beautiful barrette James gave me into the back and kissed my cheek.

Mimi and I, along with my few interns, made sure things were running smoothly. When the fountain ran out of chocolate, Mimi left my side, only to return less than two minutes later with a report that someone else was on it. She felt like a tiny dog locked on my ankle, but I couldn't shake her off, not after the way I'd been melting down periodically all week and especially all day today.

I was avoiding James, and Mimi was my buffer. He approached us, and she stayed firmly at my side with a smile, and I felt nervous flutters when his eyes dropped to my chest, then my hips, then my hidden feet. And as they swept back up to my face, I saw desire crest in his gaze.

"Ms. Hart," he said casually, and my heart did a flip.

Mimi squeezed my arm and smirked at me, and my cheeks warmed to relatively close to the temperature of the sun. "Mr. Carver, is there anything I can do for you?" I asked. I kept my tone professional, because tonight was not the time to break down crying, at least not until the event was over and most of the guests had left. Then I would allow myself to feel.

"Everything is perfect," he said as he stepped closer, and his eyes flicked to Mimi. "May we have a word?" he asked, but my throat constricted and Mimi had to speak for me.

"Actually, she's needed in the kitchen." With a polite nod, she yanked me away from him, and I was never more grateful. We had hours more of this to endure, and my heart was raw from warring against itself.

The way he devoured me, undressing me with his eyes, didn't help either. Part of me wanted to think he wasn't just objectifying me, that he was looking at me like that because he felt things for me. But I reminded myself of his stature and position. James was a very good-looking, wealthy man. He could have any woman he wanted now that he was available. He wouldn't choose someone like me.

"What are you doing," Mimi hissed, and she pulled me into the coat closet. "You're all starry eyed and drooling, and that man wanted to talk to you alone. Pull yourself together."

Shame warmed my cheeks again, and I wrung my hands together and sighed. "He's my client, Mimi. And I will have to dance with him later. I'm thinking that's when I'll do it. I'll tell him while we're dancing because there's no way he can freak out and shout at me in front of all of his friends."

I chewed the insides of my cheeks as she relaxed her grip on my arm and furrowed her eyebrows in compassion. "I thought you were waiting until after the event was over?"

I shrugged and threw my hands up in the air. "I don't know what I'm doing." Tears threatened to well up, and I turned toward the door. Waiters were carrying the silver-domed plates of food into the ballroom to serve, and I was a nervous wreck. Hiding in the coat closet wasn't going to help me at all. I thought I was doing a great job of keeping a professional demeanor, but if Mimi saw through it, James must've too.

"You may as well walk right up onto the dais and take the mic and tell the whole room. You're sweating and pale, and your hands have been shaking all day. Is it the nerves or hormones?" Her eyebrows peaked in the center now as she tilted her head to one side. "I'll help with dinner, but honestly, Ivy, you have to get this over with. Your potential customers are watching every step you take. The whole reason for coming to this party was to impress them and earn new customers for future parties, right?"

Her pinky looped through mine, and I was grateful she'd come to help me. The moral support meant more than the physical help she was being, but both were much appreciated. I squeezed her pinky and nodded, blinking back a few tears. I could do this. I was a strong woman and I didn't need a man on my arm at all. I wanted to tell James I loved him, but if it didn't work out, I knew I'd make it. My sister's support reminded me how independent I was.

We stepped back into the hallway, and I checked a few plates as they passed to make sure the quality was up to snuff. Then I peeked into the dining room to see everyone seated and dining. There was a spot next to James that was empty. It was where I assumed Barbra would typically sit, probably reserved for me. I was avoiding that, so I ducked back into the hallway and turned to see Mimi's smile.

"I'm going to grab a plate and eat. We still have the dances to deal with, and someone keeps dripping melted chocolate on the dance floor." She rolled her eyes. "Are you going to be okay for a few minutes?" she asked, and her eyes widened as she looked over my shoulder.

I slowly turned on my heel, already knowing what I would see there. James stood with one hand clasped around his other wrist, smiling at me.

"Ms. Hart, I've finished my meal and I'm ready for our dance. It's my honor each year to have the first dance before the dance floor reopens after dinner." He held his elbow out to me. "Would you do me the honor?" The way his eyes sparkled when he looked at me started to put me at ease, but anxiety rankled that peace that wanted to swell up in my chest. He was calm because he didn't know what I was about to tell him.

"You guys will be so adorable out there dancing," Mimi said Then she leaned in to speak directly into my ear. "Tell him. Everything." She emphasized the word "everything", and I knew she meant more than just the bit about the baby. We discussed how if I was going to be fully honest, I had to admit I had feelings for him, which I was terrified to do. I didn't want him to think I was lying.

"Tell me?" James said, narrowing his eyes in confusion.

But I took his arm and stepped closer to his side, forcing a smile to my face to hide the nervous flush. I ignored his question, and his hand wrapped around my hand which gripped his bicep. He led me out to the ballroom and through the tables to the dance floor. When one of his hands slid to the small of my back, it made warm pulses dance up my spine. His palm against my naked flesh did things to me, things I wanted to continue to feel.

"The evening has been fantastic, Ms. Hart."

That name. The way he said it. It felt like he possessed me. I wanted him to possess me. I wanted him to own my heart and my body, and the rest of my future.

"I'm glad you've enjoyed it." I couldn't look at him. I kept my eyes focused outward along the walls as his other hand slid up my arm to my hand. I rested my other hand on his shoulder and let him guide my body along in beat to the slow music.

"Everything looks as exquisite as you do…" I could feel his eyes boring into the side of my face, tempting me to meet his gaze. I felt a million things all at once, and yet felt so calm in his arms, as if he had the power to still the storm inside me. But I couldn't lean into that compliment. I couldn't let it make my heart feel things right now. He was saying that because he thought we were having a fling and perhaps he'd get lucky tonight. But he didn't know.

"My team worked very hard to put this together." I pressed my lips into a line and smiled at a partygoer whose eye I caught. It felt stiff and fake, because it was. I wasn't happy. I was torn up inside. I blinked my eyes rapidly and sucked in a breath. I wanted to tell him now, here on the dance floor, but the words weren't coming.

"And I think…" He paused, and I looked up to meet his eyes. "Well, what I'm trying to say is…" He faltered for words too. His tongue drew across his lower lip, and his eyes dipped to watch me bite my lip. Then he looked back into my eyes. "Please… come with me?"

There was such a pained expression of confusion and yet desire on his face, I couldn't say no. James took my hand and led me off the dance floor toward the dais. I wobbled on my heels. My palms felt like I'd dipped them in a bowl of water, and my heart pounded. This wasn't supposed to be happening. I was supposed to have a moment during our dance where I told him about the baby, about how much I loved him, and things were changing. This wasn't the plan.

He guided me toward the mic, and the singer stopped singing and directed the band to bring the music down. The volume lowered as James took the mic off the stand and smiled at his guests. My cheeks felt like I was bathed in lava, but I offered a nod of thanks to Mr. Sullivan and then tried my best not to look like a deer in headlights as I turned to address James's guests too.

"Good evening, friends and family." James stood a bit taller and his chest puffed out. "Thank you all for coming." His iron grip on my hand was crushing, but I didn't want him to let go. I felt like if he did, I'd float away. Anxiety beat on my mind. "I wanted to let you know that all of this—this whole evening, the dinner, the decorations, the band—it's all thanks to this woman right here. Ms. Ivy Hart." As he said it, he lifted my hand into the air slowly.

My head dropped, but I smiled as everyone in the room clapped and cheered. They'd obviously had a good night tonight and were grateful, but it was a bit over the top and kind of embarrassing that he put me on the spot like this.

When the cheering subsided, James continued. "I also want you all to consider her for your next event. She has been the one in charge of all of my events this year, as sadly, things in my life have changed abruptly."

The weight on my shoulders to do the right thing only got increasingly heavy. With the eyes of more than one hundred of James's peers boring into me, I felt shame and guilt multiply. This dress, this night, the way he held my hand—they weren't mine to treasure. I was a poser. A palate cleanser for him in his post-relationship status. A way he could transition from one woman to something new in the future, and I had to get off this stage before I started crying.

I started to step away, but he held me there, pulling me back to his side. "One of the changes that came about recently was this woman here by my side." I looked up at him as he stared out at his guests and wondered what the hell he was doing now. Panic seeped its way into my chest and gut, swirling around and making me feel dizzy.

"Ms. Hart hasn't just been a part of the plans for these events. She's become a part of my life." A lump formed in my throat, and I felt my palms getting even sweatier. I backed away again and shook my head. What was he doing? "Ms. Hart has become someone very dear to me."

My tongue felt like it was swelling up. It clung to the roof of my mouth, and I shook my head again as tears welled up. This wasn't happening. He couldn't be about to tell them about us, not here, not like this. He didn't know my secret. He couldn't do this to me.

"Here in front of all of you, it's my deepest heart's desire to tell you…" James turned to me, and I could've sworn there were tears in his eyes. "That I love you, Ivy Hart. You have changed my life in ways I'll never be able to explain, and—"

And I ran. I pulled my hand from his, and I turned and bolted off the stage so quickly, one of my shoes flew off, so I kicked the other off and ran faster. Tears streamed down my cheeks, and my heart felt like it would explode, and I didn't even know where to go, but I was so hot, I knew I needed air or I'd pass out. I grabbed the skirt of the long blue dress and hiked it up as I charged out the front door into the brisk February air and cried.

James loved me? But he didn't know my secret. It wasn't real. How could it be real if he didn't even know me?

33

JAMES

When Ivy took off, I felt embarrassed, but seeing the fear in her eyes as she backed away, I put my own emotions aside to think of her. I'd read her wrong. I stared after her in disbelief for a second until the hushed murmurs started, and then I cleared my throat and turned back to my waiting guests. I'd never been wrong about something like this, but there was a first time for everything. I wondered if she was embarrassed or worse. The gnawing fear that she didn't reciprocate my emotion made me feel tense as I continued.

"Well, that didn't go as planned," I said into the mic, and it earned a few chuckles, but a few of my closer friends had stern expressions on their faces. If they thought that was a shock, my next statement would really rattle them. "I know some of you are aware that Barbra and I had some problems these past few years.

"This past year has been the worst for us, and as of mid-December, we have separated." There were a few gasps, a few looks of pity or sympathy. But the weight was lifting off my shoulders as I thought of Ivy and my freedom to pursue her now. "Barbra was no longer happy to continue trying to repair our relationship, and we signed paperwork to have our marriage annulled in December."

Now that I had my announcement over with, I wanted nothing more than to go find Ms. Hart and talk about why she ran out like that. I wasn't going to let it stand for another second. I'd spent the past month in yo-yo, waiting for her to notice that I was here wanting more. She'd used work as an excuse for her business, but I knew she was purposefully avoiding me. And when her sister said to "tell me everything", I got the feeling Ivy was hiding something too. Maybe a secret similar to my own.

"I know you'll all have lots of questions, and honestly, I'd love to answer them all. But right now, I need to go find Ms. Hart and make sure she's okay. Please, continue to enjoy the wine and snacks, and enjoy the dance floor and Mr. Sullivan's music. I'll be with you again shortly." I smiled at the band, a very plastic smile, and replaced the mic, and then I left the dais as the music swelled in volume.

When I stormed into the hallway hoping to find Ivy, I saw Mimi curled around her. She appeared to be sniffling and clinging to her, and I felt bad for interrupting. Then I heard Mimi say something about "telling me" something again, and my curiosity drove me forward toward them.

"Ms. Hart?" I said, and she straightened. She was shivering, and a tear had formed a tiny ice droplet on her lower eyelash. Mimi backed away, and I slipped my tux jacket off and draped it around her shoulder. "Thank you," I told Mimi with a nod as she squeezed Ivy's hand one more time and walked away. "Are you alright?" I asked as I pulled the jacket more snugly around her shoulders.

Ivy scrubbed the tears off her cheeks and looked up at me. There was so much emotion storming in her eyes, I didn't know what to think. It didn't appear to be pain or anger. Fear, maybe, or something else...

I hated to see her so upset and hurting, especially when she looked so beautiful in that gown with her hair and makeup done. Everything about her was perfect.

"Did I go too far?" I asked her, and I stepped closer. She didn't back away from me, but her lower lip quivered. "Because I truly do love you, Ms. Hart. I've been wanting to tell you, waiting for the right moment. We have this connection, and we've never really said it to each other, but I don't want you to leave my house. It's stupid and impulsive, and I just got out of a bad relationship like you, but I'm in love.

"I know I'm way older than you, and is that it? Am I just too old, or do you think I'm too doting or controlling? Because I can—"

"I'm pregnant." Ivy's intense eyes only stormed more. They bounced around my face as her lower lip slid between her teeth and her hands wrung in front of her.

A thousand thoughts rushed through me followed by a thousand emotions. I stood there speechless, taking it in, gazing at her incredibly beautiful face. Sam's words needled at my thoughts, that she could be a gold digger out for my money. He warned me to protect myself. But the tears in her eyes, the way she was wrestling, didn't look like she was doing this for money. And if I had to be honest, it didn't matter.

What I felt for this woman was freedom. Real love. Love that was here to support her, build her up, help her, encourage her, champion her, and all with no strings attached. With no expectation of anything in return. But that didn't mean I didn't hope she'd return it to me with her own love.

"Okay," I said softly. I took a step toward her, letting that blow to my reality sink in for a second. I took her hands in mine and brought them to my lips and looked her dead in the eye and said, "It changes nothing." The hurricane pounding around my chest threatened to suck me in, but I refused to give in. I'd have stood by Barbra's side while she cheated on me repeatedly if it meant she didn't leave, but she left anyway.

This woman in front of me wasn't telling me this to hurt me. The expression in her eyes told me she'd been burdened by this secret and she needed to know I'd be there for her. How many times had I seen that expression in my former wife's eyes and I neglected it? I refused to let Ivy down in that same manner. I refused because I truly loved her.

"James, I... I'll pay back every cent of your investment. I don't want your money. I just wanted—"

"Ivy," I said, interrupting her. One of the very few times I'd said her given name aloud, and it felt right. She was shaking her head, almost as if refusing to believe this could be true. "I am in love with you." I laced my fingers through hers with one hand and pinched her chin with the other, forcing the shock of her revelation away.

"I have been waiting weeks to tell you this, and I won't let you push me away again. I don't want you to pay the money back. I don't want you to beat yourself up. I don't want you to think about anything except the fact that I love you."

"But the baby... What will people think?" Her eyes were full of tears again, and when she blinked, I brushed them away with my thumb.

"Who cares? It's a huge shock for me, I'm not going to lie. But I will take time to process my thoughts about that later. Right now, I need to know that you understand how I feel. I need to know how you feel." My own heart felt desperate for validation now. I felt a deep thirst to know she felt the same way.

When she threw her arms around me sobbing, I wrapped her in my embrace. "I do love you, James. I was just so worried. I didn't want you to think I did that on purpose. I'm not a gold digger." Her confession exploded inside my heart with such joy, I almost couldn't stand it.

I lifted her off the ground and spun her in a circle and laughed before setting her down. When her feet touched the floor, I kissed her lips and cradled her face in my palms. I had the most beautiful and amazing woman in the world here, and there was nothing in the world I wouldn't do for her.

"Come dance with me," I urged, and she smiled and nodded.

"Of course," she said, and she took my hand.

The music was fast and I was energized, and even though the idea of becoming a father this late in life was a shock, it was an adventure I knew I could take on with her by my side. We danced and laughed for hours, and the stolen kisses were a prelude to what I knew was coming when we got home. To our home, because there was no way I was letting her leave my side now.

3 4

IVY

I stood with James's coat draped around my bare shoulders and his arm around my waist as Mimi walked to his car. The stoop outside his house was lit by an overhead globe, casting a soft silhouette of our forms on the freshly falling snow. Mimi wiggled her fingers and grinned at me as she climbed into the back of his limo and shut the door. We watched it roll down the driveway until the taillights disappeared through the gate, and then he kissed my cheek.

"Let's go inside..." He coaxed toward the door, and he didn't have to work too hard at it. I was freezing in this gown and the February cold bit down on my skin.

James guided me into the house and let me keep his jacket as he took my hand and led me toward his bedroom. I paused by my room, where I knew all my things were packed and ready to go. I looked at the door cautiously and didn't know exactly where I stood. Mom was expecting me home tonight with Mimi, but James asked me to stay.

"Something wrong?" he asked, and I swallowed the knot in my throat.

"It's just..." I stared at the door of the bedroom I'd been sleeping in, and then my eyes swept up to meet his. "We have a lot to discuss..."

"Yes, we do," he said, and he opened his bedroom door and tugged me through it. When it clicked shut behind me, I felt his fingers on my shoulders as he took his jacket from me. The room was warm, the fireplace along the far wall burning. He turned me around and tossed his jacket across his dresser. "Say it again..."

"Say what?" I asked, smiling. I wasn't sure what he was getting at, and there were so many things that we had to say to each other. I didn't know which one he meant.

"Tell me you love me." His hands rested on my hips, and he backed me slowly across the room.

"I love you, silly."

"Now tell me you're making me a father." His hand slid across to my belly, and he pressed his palm there. "Tell me it's true..." A grin stretched across his face, and I couldn't help smiling too.

"I am... You are... I mean... I'm pregnant." I fumbled for words as I felt my calves press against the bed frame.

"My God, I thought things couldn't get any better, and you've gone and outdone yourself. Promise me something." His lips brushed over mine, and I smiled.

"Anything."

"We'll never avoid each other again. I am so in love with you, I want to spend every waking second worshiping the ground you walk on." His lips crashed into mine, and I opened my mouth to let him in. His tongue slid along my lips and danced with mine as I weaved my fingers into the hair on the back of his head. When he pulled away, he said, "I don't want you to leave, either. You are free to do as you please, but I want you in my bed every night."

Warmth spread through my chest, and I pulled him down for another kiss. The invitation was more than I hoped for. I couldn't believe this night turned out this way. I expected to be crying in a cab on the way home from being rejected. Not this.

"Say it..." I whispered to him, and he smirked at me because he knew exactly what I wanted him to say.

"As you wish, Ms. Hart..." My name rolled off his lips as we tumbled to the bed and his weight pinned me down.

The feel of him against me set my skin on fire, and I arched my back, needing more of him. His fingers found the zipper on my dress and with one swift movement, he had it down, exposing my bare skin to his heated gaze. He savored the sight before him, his eyes ravenous as they traveled up and down my body.

"You're so beautiful..." he breathed before dipping his head to trail hot, wet kisses down my neck. Heat flamed in my groin.

I let out a moan when his lips found their way to my hardened nipple, flicking it with his tongue as he tore off his shirt. Buttons skittered across the bed and floor, and his chest pressed against my pelvis and thighs as he sucked my nipple. He slid his hand between my thighs, and I gasped at the contact. His fingers were hot against my dampness and his touch sent electric currents through my body.

"God, I've missed this," he groaned into my ear before he pulled away. His eyes were dark with lust and desire. As he rose up and undid his pants, I readjusted myself on the bed and shimmied my panties off. When he returned to me, I spread myself for him, inviting him in.

James wasted no time pushing into me, and I moaned in pleasure as he filled me. He settled there, sinking as deep as he could, and I found his lips again. He stayed still for a moment, adjusting to my depth, and I pulled him against my body. This felt right, everything about it—him and me, this house, the baby. I was so in love.

And when he started thrusting in agonizingly slow movements, I whimpered for more. My pussy was on fire for him, screaming for release as he drew it out. His stubble scraped over my chin and his teeth bit down on my neck. One hand squeezed my right breast, and my fingernails dug into his flesh.

"Do it... God... I want to come so bad," I whined, and he chuckled, a low rumble that vibrated me to my core.

"Maybe not right now... Maybe it's a ways off... But I want you to marry me, Ivy." His confession made me moan more. The coil in my gut tightened, and I was on the edge.

My strong muscles clenched around his shaft as the glorious friction rubbed my G-spot to a frenzy. I whimpered and nodded and kissed him again and again, and he whispered, "But don't worry... I can still call you Ms. Hart if you want."

When he said my name, I detonated. The convulsions ripped through me, and I shuddered under him on the bed. As if he sensed the emotions coursing through me, he kissed me hard again. His teeth and lips and tongue devoured me, and I cried out louder than I ever had with him. James swallowed each cry of pleasure and pushed me further. The climax was intense, so much so that I almost missed the warmth that spread inside my body when he exploded.

His soft grunts in my ear as his thrusts slowed satisfied me, and he lay on top of me for a second before rolling us both over so I was draped across his chest. His arms wrapped around me firmly, and I rested my head on his chest.

Tears of joy welled up, but I blinked them back and pressed a kiss to his shoulder. Being here in his arms was more than I could ever hope for and was such a stark contrast to everything Mike had put me through. I savored the feeling of his flesh against mine and his dick inside me. So when he pulled out, I whimpered audibly, and he kissed my temple.

"Don't worry," James said, "I'll be ready to go again in twenty minutes." He started to pull away, like he was going to get up, and I snagged his hand and held him in place so he couldn't get off the bed. "What is it?"

"Did you mean it?" I asked, and I rolled to my side. He lay back down and pulled me against his body again.

"Mean what?"

"That you want me to be your wife? It's sort of sudden, isn't it?" I searched his expression and saw nothing but sincerity there.

"Of course I mean it. This isn't some rebound thing I'm going to tire of in a few months. I love you." He cupped my cheek and said, "Love at first sight is sort of sudden, isn't it?" The smile he offered me warmed my soul.

"Sudden... I think that's going to be a theme for us, because suddenly, I want you inside me again." I grinned, and he used a finger to touch the tip of my nose.

"Let me pee..." He winked at me and pulled away, and I laid my head down and closed my eyes.

Yes, better than I ever imagined....

35

EPILOGUE: JAMES

I stood at the head of the grand ballroom exactly one year after telling Ivy I loved her for the very first time, and while it was Valentine's Day, and most decorations usually looked similar this time of year, everything was different. Pride puffed my chest out a little farther this year as I looked down at the chairs organized in rows instead of around tables.

The chocolate fountain flowed, though little fingers of children would later grace it while adults danced and celebrated. Ivy's mother sat in the front row wearing a stunning purple gown, on the shoulder of which was spit up. Franklin sat on her lap, my pride and joy, my son. He was barely six months old and was already sitting up on his own.

I beamed at them, and she made his little hand wave up and down at me. I couldn't have been a prouder parent. Even in my mid-forties, I found myself loving being a father. Ivy nursed him, though I helped her throughout those rough nights, and when the business really started to take off, she hired her sister full-time as her assistant. It was great seeing them work so well together.

But today, as I stood waiting for my beautiful bride to walk down the red velvet carpet toward me, all I could think of was the life we would have together now.

Ivy and I had never been more in love. I proposed to her officially on her birthday in July and told her I didn't want to wait another second to be married to her. She convinced me to wait until after the baby was born, and when she pushed a Valentine's Day wedding, I knew it was perfect.

My eyes scanned over the cluster of our guests, only fifty, as this year's ceremony and my annual Valentine's gala were combined, and Barbra's friends had been taken off the guestlist. But Sam, who stood to my left, was never more supportive. When he saw how Ivy and I clicked, he knew it was fate too.

"Holy smokes, you're a lucky man, James," he whispered in my ear when Ivy walked in. She walked alone, with no father to escort her down the aisle. Sam offered, but Ivy was so damn independent, she said she would give herself away, which made me chuckle.

And Sam was right. I was a very lucky man. The sweetheart gown she wore accentuated her fuller breasts, large from pregnancy and now from nursing. The white silk Mikado was my idea. I loved drenching her in all the finest things because only the best was good enough for my wife. The couture gown had been designed by Isabel Marant, despite Ivy's protests. She wanted simplicity, and I wanted to unburden myself from the millions of dollars just wasting away in bank accounts.

It was totally worth it. She was phenomenal in that gown.

She held her head high as she walked toward the dais. Mimi, who stood across from me, grinned at the sight of her sister, and Ivy's eyes seemed to meet hers. For a moment, they smiled at each other until she pulled her gaze away and met mine. When she looked at me, I felt complete. It was a wholeness I had craved my whole life, one I would never take for granted.

Ivy ascended the steps and took her place across from me. She handed her bouquet of white and pink roses to her sister and then took my hands. When Franklin started to cry, she pouted a happy pout and pressed her hand to her chest, mouthing "my milk" to me, which made me chuckle. It was like her to bring some comic relief to this moment.

I wasn't a man for tears. Even at the worst moments of my life, I never let anyone see me cry. But standing here looking at her and knowing what an incredible woman she was made my eyes fill with emotion. I teared up and smiled at her, wanting to pull her against me and kiss her to show her how much she meant to me.

The minister started his prayers and readings, but we were locked in time, fixated on each other's gaze. In Ivy I'd found a friend. I'd found someone who wanted to see me do well and succeed as much as I wanted her to. I had found a strong, independent woman who was all the while capable of being intimate and bonding. I found love and I found hope.

And most of all, I found healing. The wounds of my past were irrelevant every time I looked into her eyes. She had a way of melting me down and building me back up, of challenging me to be the father and partner I should be, and she had my heart.

"Would you like to exchange your vows?" the minister asked, and Ivy nodded. She reached to Mimi's hand, and her sister placed my ring in her palm. I stretched my hand behind myself to Sam, who placed Ivy's four-million-dollar wedding band in my palm, and then we turned to each other.

"Ivy, you may go first…" The minister's nod gave her permission, and I listened intently as she cried and struggled through her vows.

"James… I know the way we met and started this relationship was anything but conventional. The day I met you was the day I moved in with you." She paused, and people chuckled. I was tempted to look at them, but I couldn't tear my eyes away from her. "James, you are my heart. You are my life. You are the good I have in this world. You taught me to love myself, and you taught me to be me. I will never, ever be able to thank you for the way you changed my life. Every day, I promise to honor your heart, to champion your dreams, and to be everything a wife and mother should be. And when I fail, I know you'll be there to pick me up. I love you."

As she finished, she slid the ring onto my finger and blinked a few tears out. Her touch was still electric. We could have sex seven times a day and it would still do the same thing to me every time.

"James," the minister nudged, and I was glad for my turn. I had been waiting months for this moment. He didn't have to tell me twice.

"Ms. Hart," I said, smiling, and she snickered and covered her mouth. "I think you know that you are my world." I sobered and offered her a very serious expression. "I tried this once before and it didn't stick, mostly because I failed at understanding what true love is. With one simple sentence, you expressed it more perfectly than anyone ever had in my entire life, and that was the moment I knew I loved you." I brought her hand to my lips and kissed her knuckles, then continued.

"I promise to cherish you. I promise you will always get to speak your mind, have your choices, express your heart. And most of all, I promise there will never be a day that you lack anything and everything you want. If you want attention, I'll clear my schedule. If you want affection, I'll pour it on you like the sweetest perfume. If you want space, I'll wait outside your door with a platter of the finest foods, waiting for you to invite me in again.

"You are my goddess, and I worship you, your heart, your passions, your body..." That one drew a hushed gasp and a few snickers from the crowd, and I finished. "And you are the only one I'll ever want for every day, the rest of my life." I held her gaze for a moment until the minister interrupted.

"Ladies and gentlemen, I would like to announce to you, Mr. and Mrs. James Carver." Then to us he said, "You may now kiss your beautiful bride." Even the priest knew she was hot.

I lifted her veil and folded it behind her head, and then I cupped both cheeks and brought my lips to hers in a heated kiss—our first of many as a married couple. Ivy kissed me back, and the entire room erupted into applause and cheers. I had never been happier in my life, and I didn't think anything could ever make me this happy again. It was all her, and my heart was now complete.

Made in the USA
Monee, IL
01 February 2025